BULBS, BEER & BISCUITS

BY READING WRITERS

ANDY BENNETT   JILLIAN BOST   MORGAN BRENNAN

FRANCES BRINDLE   GARETH CAHILL   ELOISE CURTIS

EILEEN DICKSON   RAY OFFIAH   STEVE PARTRIDGE

EMILY POWER   JULIE ROBERTS   ILARIA WARREN

ROB WICKINGS   MEG WOODWARD

Edited by MEG WOODWARD
Cover design by ILARIA WARREN
Illustrations by ELOISE CURTIS
Foreword by MEG WOODWARD

CONTENTS

FOREWORD

In bringing this book to you, I feel I must begin with a confession: I am not a native of Reading, like many of the authors in these pages are. The town has been my home for less than two years, and to begin with I could barely call it that. I was bitterly homesick for the West Midlands, where I had lived my entire life. In my eyes Reading was unfamiliar and lonely.

You see, I had an image of what I thought the town was before we were ever introduced properly. To me Reading was little more than a commuter town, on the verge of being swallowed whole by the behemoth of London – back then we all thought Cross Rail was imminent. Reading was its labyrinthine modern train station and its indomitable one-way system. It was a place where, once a year, welly-footed teenagers danced and left tent wreckage. I saw it as though through a train or car window: sliding past, grey, and unlikely to leave a mark.

I would like to apologise for my prejudice. In less than two years Reading has shown me how very wrong my presumptions were.

Reading's bones are old. The Romans may have used it as a stopping place between Calleva Atrebatum (nearby Silchester) and London, or as a trading port on the River Thames. In the 8th century A.D. it was Readingas, from the Anglo-Saxon 'Reada's People'. Its abbey was founded by Henry I in 1121, and decimated during the Reformation by his namesake, Henry VIII. But it is the Victorians who cut the cloth that Reading still wears to this day: the rows of narrow terraces in red and grey and cream-coloured brick, the primary schools with their extravagant clock towers, and the railway that wires Reading into north, south, east and west.

The Victorians, too, are largely responsible for the Three Bs which are the focus of our anthology, and for which, locally at least, Reading town is famous. Simonds brewery was founded in Broad Street in 1785; in the 1830s it was an early pioneer of India pale ale and in 1885 it became one of the first limited companies as H & G Simonds. Suttons Seeds was founded in 1806, and developed a national reputation for suppling high-quality seeds, bulbs and horticultural products. Huntley & Palmers set up trade in 1822 as J. Huntley & Son, a small biscuit and confectionary shop on London Street, but by 1900 Huntley & Palmers biscuits were sold in 172 countries.

While the companies themselves are long gone, their epitaphs still stand in brick and mortar: the brewery malthouse on Simmonds Street and the Huntley & Palmers Factory Social Club now house apartments. The Market Place where the Sutton family sold their seeds endures, hedged by a jumble of buildings new and old. Bricks built the railway embankments and sidings, so that the beer and bulbs and biscuits could be sold across the world. Bricks were plentiful and cheap: from the mid-19th century S & E Collier Ltd mined clay from the pits of Tilehurst, Katesgrove and Coley, and baked it into bricks of terracotta and 'Reading Red'.

Bricks are what bind these industries and the lives they shaped, and bricks still shape the lives of Reading's people today. The terraces are family homes, rented or owned, or Houses of Multiple Occupation where commuters, workers and students live. Some are in disrepair, neglected by their landlords; some are small and damp; the rent is high and the sales prices inflated. But they are beautiful for all of that, with their ornate lintels, moulded ornamentation and polychromatic patterning. The bricks of Reading house a wealth of people, of all colours and creeds, who drink and laugh and eat biscuits baked or bought, and who can smile at the wild mallow flowering along the River Kennet without knowing its name.

In this Anthology, Reading Writers wanted to capture the essence of what the Three Bs (four, including bricks) represent. The stories and poem herein are only rarely about Reading specifically or the industries for which the town is known. Instead, they explore what beer, bulbs, biscuits and bricks really mean in the lives lived by all of us: the comfort and ill-judgement of alcohol, the hope and renewal of a well-tended garden, the childish innocence of sugary things and the security (or lack thereof) offered by brick walls. In each piece some fragment of the spirit of our town is captured, but not all: to really know and love Reading, you must come here yourself.

We are, as ever, indebted to our Chair, Andy Bennett, for

his thoughtfulness and guidance. Thanks must also go to the Committee, for all their hard work in bringing this Anthology to fruition: Christina Koch, Gareth Cahill, Ilaria Warren, Josh Williams, Ray Offiah and Rob Wickings. But above all, thank you to the members of Reading Writers – without them, this Anthology would be a very thin volume indeed.

THE BULB

ELOISE CURTIS

IN THE FERTILE soil beneath an innocuous roundabout, the bulb stirred. Turning in its moist bed, a pale lilac shoot broke through the encasement, straining upwards towards the inviting light.

A passing beetle looked at the mauve growth and said out loud to himself: 'Well that is an unusual one. I must remember to invite Susan round for an exotic salad when it's fully grown.'

And he went on his way.

It didn't take long for the apical meristem to tease its way to the surface. With gusto it emerged into the world, full of strength, vitality and enthusiasm. The bulb from which it originated sat, pleased with its accomplishments, visions of rich foliage and vibrant flowers sparkling in its eyes.

The plant grew girth as well as height. A turgid stem with minuscule hairs bravely reached upwards, working hard to use the Nitrogen, Potassium, Sulphur and Magnesium it had been gifted by the soil, defying gravity with every inch it grew.

The plant watched. It watched as cars spun around it,

round and round in circles they went, like hamsters in a wheel. Occasionally the plant stopped and pondered:

'What is a 'car'?'

'What is a 'wheel'?'

'And What is a 'hamster'?'

Questions it yearned to be answered. The mysteries of this technicolour world were beyond fathom, the spectacular array of culture, variety and diversity, rotating and revolving around it, making him giddy and excitable.

As the sun strengthened, the plant felt brave. 'In a world where so much thrives, so can I.'

Buds formed and flourished and swelled to the size of golf balls. Tangerine petals bursting to escape their leafed prisons until they could wait no more. The fiery petals bloomed. Facing their heads towards the sunlight, they basked and revelled in their own magnificent beauty.

Yellow stamen attracted bees and butterflies.

'Why, how stunning you are, so bright and bold and blooming marvellous.' They were most complimentary.

The flowers beamed with pride, the plant beamed with pride, the bulb beamed with pride. It felt on top of the world.

Amidst the whirlwind of excitement the flower nor the plant heard the distant hum of an engine. Focussed so solely on its own self, it did not hear the sound getting closer and closer. And before the flower could turn its head, before its mouth could form the shape of an O in terror, the mower decapitated the flower. Chewing its delicately crafted flowers, its leaves, its xylem and phloem, into a mangled mess of mulch.

The destruction began and was over in a matter of seconds.

The bulb observed the devastation in abject horror. All of

its hard graft and painstaking work – obliterated. Inconsolable, the bulb wailed. It shouted, it swore, it bargained with whatever higher being to reverse the act of herbicide. It vowed revenge.

The passing beetle heard the cries of despair and commented with cynicism: Weeds. 'They're always the same, here one day and gone the next. That's just life.'

But the flowers, the plant and the bulb did not know they were a weed. All they were, was themselves.

After all, a weed is just a plant, out of place.

From the depths of the bulb's grief, despite being in the darkest of places, it experienced a light-bulb moment. Apathy turned to anger turned to ambition. The bulb began to plan.

This time, when a purple shoot erupted from its shell, it plunged downward, diving deeper into the soil, and it spread. Eking its way, searching for molecules to use as building blocks for its revenge.

Tendrils of roots moved through the soil like worms, encompassing firstly only the local vicinity, then the entirety of the roundabout, then beyond.

The bulb bided its time, it grew stronger and more resilient. The initial roots turned hard and tough like bone, the exploratory tendons reaching further and further, until they snaked and weaved under the entire town.

The passing beetle was perplexed and peeved.

'I don't know what it thinks it's doing, growing the wrong way, taking up all the nutrients, encroaching upon my territory of soil.' He tutted.

The bulb stayed silent, its network of roots in place, shoots primed.

One morning in March the town awoke to a shocking

discovery. Overnight their cars, their motorbikes, their washing machines, kettles, toasters and fridges, their strimmers, lawnmowers and sprinkler systems, their telephones, radios and televisions, and even the eensy weensy little night-lights in their children's bedrooms; were all wrapped in thick, purple, hairy, curled, plant.

Glaring flowers the size of tractor wheels radiated an amber glow from above the heads of the residents, overbearing and intimidating even the tallest of men. Leaves larger than human limbs enveloped all the electrical appliances, turning street lamps and traffic lights from a concrete jungle, into a real one.

The humans began to panic. Gathering their offspring under trembling arms in an attempt to protect them. The vines rose taller and taller like a fairy-tale beanstalk.

The bulb grinned, its appendages now in full control of the entire town. With a single word, the bulb instructed its flowers and its leaves to execute their plan.

A booming voice rumbled from beneath the ground:
'Now.'

Revealing its razor sharp teeth, the plant beheaded every human in unison. Masticating the veins, the nerves and the ligaments, turning them to mulch.

The cackle of insanity-driven revenge resounded throughout the land, brains and intestines hanging from the blood-stained mouths of each flower head. The taste of iron had whet its appetite. Now it wanted more.

NETZA

STEVE PARTRIDGE

Old Basing, Hampshire, August 1915

It was Netza Avenell's first time. The scent from her father's roses drifted across the bottom of the garden and the sun was high in a bright summer sky. When they had finished, she pushed herself up from the freshly dug soil in the new flower bed and looked at the outline of her hips, back, and shoulders imprinted into the soft earth; harmonious symmetry, like the lyric of a love song follows the contour of the melody. She giggled, then bit Jimmy Gilfeather just above his left nipple. He pulled back sharply and snapped in his guttural Scottish brogue, 'Net!'

'Jimmy, you can't go to France. Stay here with men … please, please, please.' She held him tight, locked her fingers together around the small of his back, looked into his amber eyes and pulled him close. She released her hands and ran her fingers over his high cheek bones and back through his black wavy hair.

'I'll never let you go Jimmy Gilfeather. Never.'

'You know I have to go Net. Come and see me off tomorrow. I'll be home in no time. It's nearly over.' He smiled, kissed her lightly on her open mouth and held her close to him.

Netza Avenell had known Jimmy Gilfeather for just five weeks. They'd met at a dance in Old Basing village hall in early July. He had arrived at his billet in Basing Road, Basingstoke two weeks before. Originally from the mining village of Glencraig in Fife, he was in North Hampshire to complete his battle training before departing to the front line in France. Jimmy Gilfeather was the third child in a Catholic family of eight, where three generations of men had gone down the pit.

A convoy of army vehicles were circled around the market square outside of the town hall. Most of the soldiers were in the arms of their loved ones; a heady mixture of perfume and newly polished boots hung in the hot summer air. Many of the women were weeping.

Jimmy said, 'Don't worry about me Net. I wrote to my mother last night and told her about you and said I would be home in four months.' He winked, gave her a big smile, kissed her on the lips and said, 'Look I've bought you something.'

From the top pocket of his tunic, he took out an oval gold brooch. In the centre of the brooch was a photograph of himself in the uniform of the Royal Scottish Fusiliers. He pinned the brooch to the centre of the high neck of Net's Sunday best dress. Then he put his hands around her waist and whispered. 'I'll be home in no time at all.'

'Gilfeather!' The voice of Jimmy's sergeant boomed out at him. He hauled himself up into the back of a nearby lorry, waved and blew Net a kiss.

'Bye Jimmy, bye, be careful, please be careful. I love you Jimmy. I love you.'

As the convoy drew away and rumbled down Winchester Street towards Southampton and war, Netza Avenell waved Jimmy goodbye and at the same time cupped her left hand over the brooch to protect him.

The following morning her father Steven Avenell found her crying in the kitchen after breakfast.

'I know Net. I know. Try not to think about it, come down the garden with me, we can put some bulbs in together. You can think about Jimmy when you plant them.'

Her father made planting holes with a dibber in the flower bed where two days before she had laid with Jimmy. Net followed behind him, dropping the iris bulbs into the holes and backfilling them with earth, tears, and thoughts of when she would see him again.

Her father said, 'They are Royal Blue with a bright yellow dash down the centre of each petal. They will look lovely when they're in full bloom. Come on, let's go and see if mum's made some tea.'

Loos, Northern France, 7.00am 25th September 1915

Private Jimmy Gilfeather and his comrades leaned against the wall of the trench, their rifles by their sides, bayonets fixed, flannel gas-masks in their hands, waiting for the inevitable order. He finished off his last slice of the homemade ginger cake Net had sent him from England and looked down the line of the trench wall opposite. Twenty yards away a black, grey, and white cloak of crows, jackdaws and magpies were feeding on the body of a waggon horse which had been ripped open by a German shell. The birds were feeding in a frenzy, bobbing, and weaving in and out of the carcass, jabbing, stabbing, and tearing at its heart and liver. Their bodies and bloodied heads clashed like boxers in the final round of a big fight.

Wheeling in a clear sky above them were eagles and buzzards positioning themselves to glide down and steal the spoils of war from them. There wouldn't be a fight, just some token snapping of beaks and flapping of wings. When it came to a carcass the corvids would always defer to the raptors' superior weaponry, returning later for the leftovers when their appetites had been sated.

Jimmy turned away from the carnivorous avarice and pulled himself up the trench so he could just peek over the top without exposing his head. Fifteen minutes earlier a labyrinth of snaking pipes had dispensed a green-yellow cloud of chlorine gas from the British trenches towards the German lines. The cloud was now three quarters the way across the divide between the two armies.

Corporal Jock McIntyre's voice boomed out down the trench. 'Listen up my bonny boys! It's our turn now. Gas masks on and pick up your rifles.'

The lance jack next to Jimmy said, 'Here's to breakfast tomorrow, son, and a dram in Sauchiehall Street when we all get home.'

Two minutes later Corporal Jock McIntyre together with hundreds of other officers and NCO's gave the order to attack. Jimmy Gilfeather and eight thousand of his comrades were up and out of their trenches, running across four hundred yards of open ground towards the German lines when the wind changed direction, sending the smell of bleach from the chlorine gas back towards them. As they ran forwards, the gas penetrated their ineffective flannel gas masks so they couldn't see out of them. Jimmy started to choke. He panicked, pulled off the mask, urinated and soaked his trousers. As he tried to run, the last sound he heard was the death rattle of German machine guns.

A second later he was cut down and torn open. Another man, for no-man's land. In just ten minutes of war, three thousand, seven hundred, and sixty-three officers and men were slaughtered. Six, every second.

~

Old Basing, Hampshire, The mid 1950s

My auntie Net wasn't my auntie. She was my mother's friend and fourteen years older than her. Although I called her auntie Net, she was more like a grandmother to me. She was in truth my godmother and her husband, Alf Vince, was my godfather. I was born almost bereft of grandparents in January 1948. Only my mother's father was living. He'd remarried and my mother, the youngest by three years in a family of six, didn't get on with her stepmother. So, Net and Alf, childless themselves, became my surrogate grandparents.

Visits to their bungalow in Old Basing were, for me, everything to look forward to when I was growing up. The bungalow had belonged to Net's parents and she had lived there for the whole of her life, Alf moving in with them after he married her. The pair of them fussed over me and filled me up with home cooking. Net would say to my mother, 'Roger's looking peaky, Sally. He's underfed.' Potatoes, carrots, broccoli, cauliflower, and runner beans, all from their own large garden; home-killed pork, bacon, and gammon, from a relative in the village; rabbit and trout taken from farmers' fields and the nearby river Loddon. Raspberries from their own canes were served in jelly with condensed milk. Net would look at Alf and say, 'Chummy, give Roger some more jellied raspberries and condensed milk. He looks like he's got room for it.'

When my father joined Alf in the kitchen, or they went outside to the look at the garden, my mother and Net would go into a huddle and talk in whispers. Sometimes Net would take something out of her handbag, hold it in her hand so I couldn't see it and they would both look at it intently and become very quiet. Carefully I would try to creep behind them to get a look at what was in Net's hand. But she would quickly slip it into her bag and say, 'Not for little boys', laugh, kiss me on the cheek and find me a Murray Mint from the depths of her handbag.

As I got older, I spent less time with them and was encouraged to join my father and Alf for walks around the garden where they would have deep conversations about the condition of the loam, their favourite varieties of runner beans, spring onions, and sprouting broccoli. There were roses and irises at the bottom of the garden, and poppies Net had planted next to them in remembrance of all the young men who had died in the Great War.

Their garden was a magical place for me. The quarter acre plot was enclosed by a six-foot privet hedge; it had plum and apple trees and a couple of tumbledown sheds full of ancient gardening tools and wooden wheelbarrows with cast iron wheels. Blackbirds, thrushes, and squadrons of sparrows flew in and out of the trees, making a living for themselves and their families from two large vegetable plots on both sides of the back section of the garden. There was a lawn opposite the kitchen window through which at night, Uncle Alf told me, if you sat quietly in the dark and the moon was bright, you could see foxes making their way across to a gap in the hedge which led to next door's garden.

My mother told me Net had taken a long time to recover from the loss of her Scottish soldier and she was thirty-two when she started seeing Alf.

She said, 'I was fourteen and had just started my apprenticeship with Thomas Burberry. My mother told me it was good I could join Burberry, because she could arrange for Net to be my supervisor. She told me Net was reckoned to be the best supervisor in the factory. Although I was a lot younger than her, we spent a lot of time together. She was like an elder sister to me. We were at Old Basing village fete together when she met Alf:

'Look at that nice little man over there, Sally. What do you think of him?'

'Mum told me his parents run the village laundry down Maple.'

'From that point your Uncle Alf never stood a chance. He was destined to be Net's husband.'

When I was eleven Net and Alf taught me to play cribbage. I would partner my father and over the years we would have epic games on Boxing Day. When the count occurred in the card play, Net and Alf would come out with little rhymes and sayings to help the scoring along. If somebody laid a card to increase the score from twenty-nine to thirty one, he would say, 'Two's in time for two.' Or if the count were twenty-six and the last two cards laid were fives, should another five be laid Net would say, 'fives awake for eight, peg 'em up Chummy', when the total had reached thirty-one.

After a few Christmas drinks Net's sayings could become bawdy. If a player had a jack in their hand of the same suit as the turn up card, she would say, 'One for his nob and up he goes like a rocket.' Or, if Alf failed to win a game by one point, she would say, 'You died in the hole Chummy', chuckle, look at me and wink. I would look back at her with a straight face because I was too young to understand the jokes.

Alf would reply stoically, 'Children present, Net. Children present.'

Sometimes she would kiss me on the cheek and say, 'You're picking this game up well Rog. The soldiers used to play crib when they were in the trenches in the First World War.' Just for a second her smile would drop away, then it would return, and she would say, 'Perhaps you might be a soldier when you grow up.'

My mother would chip in at once and say, 'No he won't Net! Too many of them don't come back!'

My mother was seventy-six when Net died, aged ninety in July 1987, just two years after Alf had passed on. When we were going through her possessions together, we found a wooden box with a marquetry inlaid lid. The box contained a gold brooch with a celluloid cover about the size of a two-pound coin. Inside the brooch there was a black and white photograph of a soldier in uniform. My mother ran her finger across the cover, and it sprang off to reveal three photographs inside: the soldier, one of Net, and a third one of a small girl, under the age of one, in a silk smock. The picture of Net was taken when she was about nineteen. Pinned to the high neck of her dress is the brooch we were looking at, the photograph displayed was of the little girl.

My mother sat up quickly, surprised to see the photographs, 'Oh, look, she kept them. All those years. She kept them. I never knew. She told me she ... Oh, I wonder if Alf saw them. I haven't seen these since you were ... six or seven.'

'Who is the soldier, mum?'

She stared at my amber eyes and my black wavy hair, then said slowly, 'Jimmy Gilfeather, Rog. He was Net's boyfriend when she was eighteen. He was killed in the Great War.' She stared into the middle distance and took in a deep breath which seemed to go on forever.

'Rog ... he's your grandfather.'

'My grandfather ...? So Net is ... was ... my grandmother?

She nodded her head slowly.

'Yes ... Net was your grandmother.'

At first, she looked at me, then she broke eye contact and stared over my shoulder. Her cheeks were grey, drawn in, her eyes dull and sad.

'I should have told you ... I just couldn't do it ... not when she was alive.'

I looked back at her prominent cheek bones and glanced down at the pictures of the soldier and the child.

'So ... the little girl ... is ... you mum?'

Tears started to roll down her cheeks.

She nodded her head again. 'She told me when I was fifteen, a year into my apprenticeship ... but we had to keep it a secret. Alf was never to know. When Net told her mother she was pregnant, she was sent to relatives in Wiltshire to have me. When I was born, I was given to close family friends of Net's parents who brought me up. My Mum and Dad. Your granddad and his first wife, well at least the man you called granddad. Her parents thought nobody would marry her if she had a child, but they wanted her to see her baby and their grandchild grow up. So, they paid my mum and dad to bring me up. That's the truth Rog … Jimmy Gilfeather was your grandfather and Net was your grandmother. My real Mum.' She put her arms around me and rested her head on my shoulder.

'Sorry Rog … I know I should have told you a long time ago.'

'Does Dad know?'

'No, he doesn't know. I couldn't tell him; he was too close Alf.' She took a deep breath and wiped the tears from her cheeks. 'Let's take a walk down the garden. I want to show you something.'

When we reached the bottom of the garden there was light breeze blowing. The red heads of the poppies were bent over like cardinals on their way to mass and the irises looked like a perfect cloudless sky with flashes of summer lightning.

'Beautiful aren't they, Rog.' She pointed at the flowers, hesitated and took a deep breath, 'Look … I was conceived there … Jimmy Gilfeather and Netza Avenell made me, right there, just where those poppies are growing, next to the irises.'

We looked at the poppies and the irises for a few moments then turned and took a slow walk back up the garden path towards the bungalow, quietly reminiscing about Net and Alf. How nice they had been to me and how I would never forget visiting them on Boxing Days when I was a child. My mother opened the back door and I followed her into the kitchen, where she started to fill the kettle to make some tea. When the kettle was full, there was, for a moment, a cathartic silence. Then I heard a voice coming from the dining room.

'Fifteen two, fifteen four, fifteen six and six is a clock. Peg 'em up, Chummy.'

THE BULB

ILARIA WARREN

MARKET PLACE IS HEAVING this morning, as if the early March sun brought new energy along with its warmth. I can just spot the flower seller in the corner, the bright bouquets drifting in and out of vision as I weave my way across the square. I keep my pace steady, careful not to bump into other market goers.

Their conversations buzz through the air, random words catch my ear; did I just hear my name then?

One voice, the paperboy's, shouts louder than the others. Hard to believe such a young boy's voice could rise up and reach everyone in the square. Purposeful, calling me to attention, to his newspaper, shouting about The Factory Act. He says the Act will restrict work hours for women and children. That means a better future for the next generation. I let my smile widen as I wave the boy hello.

I wish I'd worn my light clothing. After weeks of bright but cold days, I didn't trust this morning's sun and went for winter clothes instead. But there's nothing I can do about that now. There's a certain comfort about the thick plaid. It's like a shroud.

I breathe in and let the flowery scent guide me and steady my step. This place is my escape, with its colours and scents, St. Lawrence's church towering over us, sheltering us from the elements.

I needed fresh air. The house feels stuffy at the moment, I get short of breath just walking into the hall. I can't talk to the maids, they look up to me as their superior. Especially the scullery maid, she doesn't miss a chance to gossip about anything that moves. I've been eating more just to stop myself from blurting it all out.

That's true, I've been lonely. And sick. Very sick. And the smell of flowers makes me dizzy. But the master said to get the flowers an exact shade of blue.

I know which one he wants.

'What can I do for this young lady with the lovely blue eyes?'

I feel my cheeks sting, I instinctively blink a couple of times, 'Oh, I just wanted to buy some Felicia seeds, please.'

He raises both eyebrows, as if I'd asked for something new to him, 'Felicia? Nah … Not the right time of year.'

My face must say it all, because he studies me, then realises I genuinely don't know and he proceeds to explain, 'If you sow them now, they may not germinate.'

'Of course. I don't have much experience with gardening I'm afraid.'

He tilts his head to one side, a knowing smile on his face, 'should have asked the gardener to give you some advice. Young girl like you.'

I look away, 'Not that young. I'm twenty-two next month.'

He picks up some seeds and shows them to me, 'You wanna try these lovely Dahlias; it's the right time of year. Beautiful, they are, bright red, will make the garden look stunning. Especially on a nice sunny day.'

I roll my eyes, 'I'm sure the master said it has to be blue.'

'You don't wanna plant those seeds now. You want to wait until the last frost for those. Tell you what, I'll give you a bag of the Felicias and one of Dahlias for now. How about that?'

He still hasn't wiped that ridiculous smile off his face. The gigglemug.

I hesitate over which seeds to choose. It's the blue that got my master's attention, and it's blue that will adorn the flowerbeds. It's already a done deal, no matter the time of year. The scent gets stronger. The white, the lilac and red gets to my head. The colours blur and expand like watercolour …

'Are you alright love?'

The stallholder's foghorn voice brings me back to the market. A couple of people are staring at me.

I can feel my cheeks tingle, 'I'll have both, please.'

I take the bags, holding my breath to avoid breathing in the scent. I feel faint, but don't want to cause a scene. I don't want a reputation, and Mrs Wakefield to find out from someone else's maid or gardener. I have the household's standards to uphold.

I pride myself in being the best housekeeper I can be. I am hard-working, loyal. So loyal. Mr Wakefield will tell you that and more. The house and its people are all my life. I have no life outside of it.

Mr and Mrs Wakefield, the masters, were clear on that –

no distractions, no followers. And I've been true to my word. Mr Wakefield is the only man in the house.

The only man I've spent time with.

I look down and grin at the soft bump under the thick plaid of my dress; no matter the season, some seeds aren't meant to be sown.

ALE, SEED & STONE

ROB WICKINGS

I HEARD Redstone Ray long before I found him. Grunts, barks, spat-out curses in long-dead languages. The Crosswater Wizard had always been an impatient man. Whatever he was up to had clearly broken the thin boundary of calm sketched around his soul.

The Caversham Court Allotments are tucked at the back of the old home of England's Greatest Knight. Now little more than a floor plan in concrete, William Marshall's place still held an aura that drew the people of Reading to its gardens, to sip tea by the river while perched on the stone blocks sketching out his old kitchens and drawing rooms.

A rusted wrought-iron gate at the top of the terrace gave access to the Allotments. The land was impossible to get to from the road. The plots were cramped, the facilities limited. There was a ten-year waiting list to get onto it. The Caversham Court Allotments had something special, drawing gardeners like bees to blossom.

At first, I couldn't see Ray. There was, though, plenty of evidence as to his whereabouts. From a far corner of the site, clods of earth flew into the air. Spurts and flares of green light sputtered about, licking the air with electrical tongues. A tiny raincloud, no bigger than a football, boiled to life six feet over a stand of cabbages to my left. It went black, dumped a sudden bucketful of rain over the brassicas, then vanished.

'Ray?' I shouted. 'Are you here?'

The racket ceased. One last fist of dirt hovered in the air for a second, then drifted gently down. A tousled, beard-tangled head popped up over a tilting wicker screen. A pair of red plastic Aviators perched on the end of his nose. Even across the Allotments, even through the shades, I could see the simmering green of his eyes.

'Bout time,' he said. His voice was gravel and brick-dust. 'Got the stuff?'

I nodded and walked over.

Behind the screen, chaos reigned. Ray's plot was three times larger than any other on the Allotment and completely clogged with weeds. Nettles, ivy and brambles tangled about each other in an impenetrable net. Ray glared at me as I crossed into the space, then bent back to his task. He slashed at the greenery double-handed, a trowel in one hand and a kitchen cleaver in the other.

'I only did this the other week. Now, look at it. Bugg'rin' spiky bugg'rs.' He swung at a knotted clump of brambles, which whipped back and swatted him hard in the face. Ray bellowed in old Norse, something about mothers and manure.

'Bugg'r this,' he said. He dropped the tools and raised his left hand in a claw. Green fire fizzed between his fingers. 'Burnin' time.'

'Ray. Ray, no.' I jumped in front of him, putting myself

between the wizard and the weeds. 'Use spite-fire here and you might as well salt the earth. Nothing will ever grow again.'

I locked eyes with him, his green against my brown. 'Just calm down. You asked for my help. Let me give it to you.'

Ray's expression softened. He flicked his fingers and the spite-fire flew into sparks, drifting away in the breeze.

'So help,' he said.

I took a deep breath, held it. I raised both hands, fingers already forming the right shapes. I settled my feet firmly in the rich ground. I closed my eyes and saw the garden clearly. Every plant, every leaf, every fruit, every root. They spoke to each other in rustles and whispers, the creak of branches against the wind, the soft vibrations of growth and decay.

Into that murmuration, I placed a request, a favour. The garden considered it, and granted my boon, along with a message to my companion.

Gently, without fuss, the snarl of plant life in Ray's plot retreated, twining back and away, some shrivelling, some simply bending and flattening. In moments, ill-kept beds and planters that had been hidden under the mass of greenery emerged like submarines from the depths. Four raised beds in a square, with a brickwork knot in the middle.

'There,' I said, as the plants settled quietly into place. 'All you had to do was ask nicely. Oh, and the garden wants you to know, don't leave it so long to visit next time. When did you last do any pruning?'

Ray frowned. 'Few weeks,' he said. 'Quite a few weeks.' He thought for a moment. 'Nineteen thirty-seven.'

I shook my head. 'You deserved that slap from the brambles, I'd say. Look after your garden or it'll take advantage.'

'Bugg'rin' earth magic. Never understood it. Gimme stone and water any day.'

'It's simple, Ray,' I said. 'Even the mortal-folk get it.'

'Hmph. Put a stick in the ground then there's a flower? Don't make no sense to old Ray. We's wasted enough time. Let's be at us task.'

We crossed into the centre of the square. Ray let one booted toe rest on the brickwork knot and let out a contented sigh. 'That's better,' he said. 'You know where you are with red stone. Fire, water, good clay, bound and given purpose. Solid. Dependable. Stays where you put it.' He side-eyed me. 'Don't go rompin' off without permission.'

I ignored him and emptied the pockets of my jacket. First my trowel, silver-bladed, horn-handled. I stuck it in the soft patch of earth right at the middle of Ray's knot. Then I retrieved the rest. In one hand, a brown glass bottle topped with a brass crown. In the other a fat bulb as round as an onion. I handed the bottle to Ray. 'Open that.'

I bent to the knot, and dug into the ground. Three trowel-fuls of earth gave me a hole deep enough to plant the bulb. I patted dirt gently over it and smoothed everything down. I straightened, knees clicking.

There was a hiss of gas as Ray opened the bottle. He used his teeth, lifting the crown free with his strong molars before spitting it across the plot.

'Heathen,' I said.

'Bloody right. Bit early for a drink, t'ain't it?'

I squinted at the sky. 'Sun's over the yard-arm.' I gestured and Ray handed the bottle over. Carefully, I poured a third of the contents onto the bulb. The golden liquid fizzed as it landed.

Then I took a gulp, letting the cool bitterness slide down my throat. I'd had to test a lot of ale before finding the right one for the job. Research is important. North of the river, at Dunsden Green, I'd finally hit the jackpot. Reading Best, of course.

I handed the bottle to Ray. 'Down in one.' He didn't need telling twice. One swallow emptied the bottle. I took his free hand and fixed my gaze on him, brown on green.

'Ale and stone,' I said. 'Plant and earth. Grown and made. Root and branch. Hand and tool.' I closed my eyes and saw the bulb, the spark within it. The plant, the red stone surrounding it, the golden ale watering it.

'Beer, bulb, brick,' I said. 'Balance.'

The air shivered. A thrush singing lustily in a tree nearby went quiet. The traffic noise from St. Peter's Hill likewise snuffed. I looked at our hands. For a second, the bones were visible through the flesh.

Then the thrush started up again, and the hum of the cars on the hill bulged out into the air.

'That it?' said Ray.

'That's it.'

'Now what?'

'Now? This is earth magic, Ray. You plant. Then you water. Then you wait. Then you see what you get.'

'So you don't know if it worked.'

'Not yet,' I paused, then smiled. 'But I have a good feeling.'

Ray was still looking at the knot, as if willing a great green rope of growth to come bursting out of the ground. I touched his elbow, and was surprised to feel him startle.

'Don't seem like much,' he said, 'consid'rin' what's at stake.'

I looked at him properly then. The Crosswater Wizard seemed pale, thinner than I remembered, more grey in his beard. The last six months had taken a lot out of him. Holding back the worst of it, hiding the true nature of the threat to us all. A heavy burden for anyone to bear. Typical of Redstone Ray to leave it till the last moment to ask for help.

'You'd be surprised what plants can do,' I said. 'That's part of the fun of it.'

Ray grunted, sniffed at the air. 'Smells different,' he said. 'Purer.'

'There. See? A bit of time in the garden will always bring a fresh perspective.'

Ray gave the faintest of smiles. Then his belly gurgled, growling like a bear. 'Beer on an empty stomach,' he said. 'Knew I should've had breakfast.'

I dug in my pockets once more. There. The fat, tube-shaped packet crinkled faintly. I pulled it out and untwisted the top, offering it to Ray.

'Never mind,' I said. 'Here. Have a biscuit.'

NOT JUST CRICKET

MORGAN BRENNAN

IN A SOFT SPRING BREEZE, lilac and purple crocuses swayed their pretty heads at Henry Belcher – who had three minutes before he was dead meat. That was all the time it would take for her to reach him. He lay prone on the grass with his stomach contents before him and the bitter taste of regret in his mouth. He had crossed a boundary – and now he would pay the price. How had it come to this when the day had started so perfectly …?

'Henry, do you remember where I put my hat? The Ascot one?'

'Yes, darling, it's in the conservatory.'

'You're a brick. Don't know what I'd do without you.'

'Yes, darling.'

'Isn't it wonderful? Our Tom, getting a First, and now captain of the University's first eleven. I'm so proud.'

'Well, he's a bright lad, can't think who he gets it from.'

'Now, have you got everything, Henry?'

'Picnic hamper and blanket – check. Large parasol –

check. Beer and wine – check. Oh, binocs – check. Yes, I think that's all.'

'Have you got the biscuits?'

'Of course, darling, they're in the hamper.'

'Good, let's go then. I don't want to be late in case he's batting first.'

The Jaguar XJ6 4.2 litre engine growled away from the pristine driveway of the Belcher's residence that spring morning. The annual cricket match between Reading University and Eton was taking place at Huntley and Palmers, Kensington Road recreation ground. Jane Belcher, head-hunter and tiger mother was at the wheel. Henry, insurance claims assessor, was firmly in the passenger seat.

'No need to hurry. Watch out for those cyclists, Jane.'

'Bloody old fools in lycra. Get on the pavement!'

'They are allowed on the road, darling.'

'Damn nuisance these days.'

'Take a left here.'

They sped into the car park and straddled two spaces.

'Right, come along, Henry. Let's bag the best spot.'

'There won't be many watching, darling; it's not like the old days.'

'I don't care; we're grabbing the best place to watch our son.'

The Belchers unloaded their booty and claimed a prime piece of England's green and pleasant land beside the boundary and within sight of the cricket pavilion and scoreboard. On the field of play, thirteen urgent young men in whites fought for ascendancy over a small leather ball. Two umpires, bent with age, looked after proceedings with the wisdom of Solomon. Above, a perfect blue sky and golden orb blessed them all. This was England, their England.

'Look there's Tom, opening the batting. Wave at him. Why isn't he waving back?'

'He's trying to concentrate, Jane. The burden of captaincy and all that.'

'Wouldn't it be wonderful if he got a hundred today?'

'Bloody marvellous, darling. Now, where's the beer?'

The car park was still half empty when a Bentley, the size of a small country, drove in and parked next to the Belcher's vehicle.

'Oh bloody hell it's the Rhodes–Browns.'

'Their lad must be playing for Eton, darling.'

'Oh yes, Toby. Dim as a dipstick.'

'Watch out, they're coming over here, but hang on, that's not Sylvia.'

Guy Rhodes-Brown, property entrepreneur and God knows what else, marched across to them. A young woman struggled behind him with a large hamper and two camping chairs.

'Hurry up, Natasha. Haven't got all day.'

'Guy, what a delight to see you here. We wondered if Toby might be playing. But where's Sylvia?'

'Migraine. Natasha's our new au pair. When Sylvia pulled out, I suggested introducing her to the great game. She's very sporty. Natasha, these are two very dear friends, Henry and Jane Belcher. Their lad Tom's on the other team. Natasha's from Poland, studying English and Sports Science or something.'

'How do you do, Mr and Mrs Belcher. A pleasure to meet you.'

'Well that's very good English, Natasha; now would you like a beer or wine?'

Conviviality broke out as hampers were opened and food and drink, and more drinks were consumed. Then Guy took a fateful phone call.

'Sorry folks, Sylvia needs me to take her to the docs. Look after Natasha while I'm gone will you, Henry. Teach her some of the finer points of the game. Back later.'

'OK, love to Sylvia.'

'Yes, I hope she gets better soon, Guy. Hand me those binoculars, Henry.'

'This beer's awfully good; here you are.'

'Oh, good shot, did you see that, Henry? Tom's up to forty-five already. This wine tastes bloody awful though. I'm going to the pavilion to see if I can't find something better and I think I can see Tom's maths tutor.'

Jane tottered off with binoculars and hat leaving Henry in the company of Natasha.

'Hope this isn't boring you?'

'Oh no, I love your cricket. It's so English. The young men in their whites. It's how you say – quite sexy. But I like older men too.'

'Umm, yes, would you like another beer, Natasha? It's a Reading craft beer, from Loddon I think. Quite strong mind you.'

'Sure, Henry, in Poland we call this piss water – but it's very nice though and from London.'

'Err yes. Now, what do you know about cricket?'

'All I know is that there are two sides. One out in the field and one in. Each guy that's in the side goes out, and when he's out, he comes in and the next guy goes in until he's out. When they're all out, the side that's out comes in and the side that's been in goes out and tries to get those coming in, out.'

'Well, that's bloody brilliant, Natasha – have another piss water.'

The game was afoot as the sun reached its zenith.

'I am getting rather hot, Mr Henry, can I come under the parasol with you?'

'Course you can. Jane will be a while.'

'Thank you, that's better. Mr Rhodes-Brown is generous man but very direct if you get my meaning. Am thinking of moving out. Can do ironing and make beds, Mr Henry.'

'I'm not sure Mrs Henry would approve, Natasha.'

'Is a shame … so tell me more cricket. How you bowl a maiden over?'

'Ah well, it's six times without scoring.'

'Mr Rhodes-Brown, he tries many times. Tries too hard. But you, I think you are a soft signals type of guy. You charm the ladies. Another piss water, please.'

'Ahem, well, in cricket, Natasha, they use soft signals on TV when they can't make up their mind.'

'I've made up my mind about you. This piss water's stronger than I thought. I think I am going to kiss you, Mr Henry.'

'Ah now, I don't think that would be advisable, here.'

'Too late, Mr Henry.'

The lovely Natasha slumps over Henry and lands a smacker on his lips. He instinctively holds onto her youthful body. From the pavilion balcony, a pair of binoculars is trained upon them. Jane screams.

'Henry, you bastard, I'm coming down!'

Suddenly Henry feels sick. He rolls out from under the

inebriated Natasha and staggers away to throw up and then fall flat on his face in a patch of lilac and purple crocuses. He lies there, awaiting certain death.

More than three minutes pass and he's still alive.

'Henry, get up. I'm not going to kill you. Natasha's drunk and you're a silly man with a middle-aged crisis. When I saw you and her together, I lost my rag, but then I realised something. It was like a lightbulb moment. I realised it's been all about Tom these last twenty-one years and we've lost something special between us. I know Tom will be fine now. He'll be a success and go off and work for some tax-avoiding multi-national in London. He'll marry a sweet middle-class girl and have two-point-four children and live in a leafy suburb with no cycle lanes. But us? What about us? We need to relight the fire, Henry. Get up, I'm taking you home.'

'I'm sorry, darling, it's all my fault.'

'Nonsense, Henry. Blow the cricket and let's go home. I'll make it up to you.'

'But Tom?'

'Never mind, Tom. I'll wear that negligee you bought me – twenty-two years ago.'

'Oh, I see. In that case …'

The two middle-aged, middle-class parents linked arms and walked unsteadily back to the car park.

'Are you sure you can still drive, darling?'

'Of course, I've only had a couple of glasses of wine.'

'You will watch out for cyclists though won't you, darling?'

'Bugger cyclists.'

At that moment, across the green and pleasant playing fields of Huntley & Palmer, a handsome young man threads a perfect cover drive through the privileged ranks of Eton's outfielders to the boundary. Tom Belcher looks up and waves his bat towards his ecstatic teammates acknowledging his hundred. Then he turns to where his parents were supposed to be only to see them in the distance, arm in arm, walking back towards their car. For a moment he frowns, and then a broad grin cracks his young face. Bright boy, that Tom Belcher.

HOLY ORDERS

GARETH CAHILL

'MAY you walk in the light of the Gods,' Brother Jonns said, his arms outstretched towards the congregation in front of him and his voice resonating around the temple.

'May it banish the shadows from our souls,' the congregation replied in unison.

Brother Jonns bowed his head, drawing the Holy Day temple service to a close. A gentle hum began to rise through the faithful, a hundred different conversations blossoming as they began shuffling through the pews to make their way outside. Brother Jonns turned and began to reset the altar for the next service, gently humming to himself.

The metallic chink of iron spurs on the hard flagstone floor cut through the murmur of the departing crowd. One set of spurs, although they were accompanied with the sharp click of other footfalls in riding boots. Brother Jonns kept at his task even when the footsteps came to a stop just short of the dais where he was.

'Sheriff,' Brother Jonns said after a pause.

'It brings me joy that the Gods allow you to feel my presence.'

'The Gods have nothing to do with it. There are so very few who would enter the temple so adorned,' Brother Jonns replied. He closed his eyes and grimaced before taking a breath and turning around. He met the sheriff's gaze, then looked at the spurs on the sheriff's boots and those of the two City Guard flanking him. 'Your carriage waiting for you outside?'

'Oh, come now. There's no need to be like that. Now that the Gods commune directly with the Chamberlain, as well as your Brotherhood, we all benefit.'

Brother Jonns gave the sheriff a smile but shook his head and returned his attentions to resetting the altar. 'And you are here today for our benefit? Or yours?'

The sheriff gave a chuckle that was echoed by his guards but was as empty as the pews in the temple now were. 'You have to admit, Brother, that since the Gods started to speak to our Chamberlain your temples have never been so full.'

'You mean since the Chamberlain outlawed alcohol as it was an affront to the Gods?' asked Brother Jonns.

'Brother, no need to sound so bitter. We all miss having a small dram on occasion. But it was the Gods that spoke to him and proclaimed their sadness at their faithful being overly influenced by sinful alcohol. It does make me wonder why the Gods chose him to speak to and not, say, the Council of Abbotts. Anyway, you have many more coming to your services now, and I dare say with much rounder purses too.'

Brother Jonns cocked an eyebrow and glanced over to where an acolyte had placed the collection baskets from the service.

'In return for this newfound devotion of the people, the Chamberlain has agreed a new levy of forty percent.'

The fresh candle that Brother Jonns had been holding in his hand snapped in two.

'I've got quite the schedule to keep today, Brother, as I'm sure you have too. We could say a rough forty percent this week and work out what's missing later and make up for it in next week's levy.'

Brother Jonns wasn't aware exactly when his hands had balled into fists, one with half a candle sticking out of the bottom, but his knuckles had turned white.

'That has not been agreed,' commanded a voice from behind the curtains at the back of the dais. Brother Jonns took to his knee in reverence. As well you know, Sheriff.'

Abbott Kayzen, flanked by two Holy Guard, walked out onto the dais, gesturing Brother Jonns to rise from his knee. The sheriff and his guard stepped backwards at the Abbott's approach. 'This is the second temple I have found you in peddling the same untruth. I have told you once and I am telling you again, the Council has not agreed to anything with the Chamberlain yet. The levy stands at ten percent.'

From inside his red woollen robes the Abbott took out a purse and absently tossed it towards the sheriff. The coins chinked as the sheriff had to stagger and stretch to catch it, even then almost fumbling.

'That should cover this temple quite adequately,' said Abbott Kayzen, marching down the steps of the dais, Holy Guard beside him in perfect unison. He levelled a finger at the sheriff, 'I will not be telling you a third time. The Holy Guard now stand with the other Brothers in the temples across the city, you will find they will not tell you either. Now get out.'

Abbott Kayzen gave a nod and the two Holy Guard marched forward, hands on sword hilts, ready to draw if needed. Their step forwards was deliberate, pushing the sheriff and his men backward with the strength of their presence alone, leaving little grace for them to turn on their heels. The sheriff glanced back as they were encouraged out of the main temple doors, his brow furrowed, and lips bent in a sneer. His gaze was met flatly by the Abbott's own.

'Abbot, you honour me with your presence,' Brother Jonns said.

'Nonsense,' the Abbot replied as he watched the Holy guard close and lock the temple doors. My presence has nothing to do with honour. It has everything to do with our survival.'

'Abbott?'

'Take me down to the catacombs.'

Brother Jonns lit the torches ensconced on the walls from the lamp he had brought down into the catacombs with him. The scent of the old pitch tickled his nostrils. The torches were changed when necessary; however it had been a long time since anyone had been this far down in the catacombs: there were statues and figures that Brother Jonns did not recognize.

'Forgive me, Abbott,' Brother Jonns said, 'but why are we so far down?'

'We're away from prying eyes and ears,' replied the Abbott as he walked close to the east side of the chamber, periodically tapping on the ancient brickwork. 'Let me ask you, Brother, do you believe that the Gods have spoken to the Chamberlain?'

'Truth be told?'

'Always, Brother. Always.'

'I have my doubts,' Brother Jonns said with a sigh that took a weight from his shoulders. 'The holy texts have always pointed towards visions and symbols rather than direct words. I do question, in my own mind of course, why would the Gods suddenly commune with the Chamberlain and not one of the Abbotts?'

'Have you heard of the saksa pipe?' Abbott Kayzen asked, wrapping his knuckles against more bricks along the wall.

'Only from a few wives and mothers claiming it has taken their husbands and their sons,' Brother Jonns replied. 'From what I gather it is an expensive and rare leaf to obtain. Forgive me, Abbott, but are you suggesting that the Chamberlain is imbibing in the saska pipe?'

'Oh, no, no, I'm not suggesting it at all. It has been relayed to me by many in his inner court. His outlawing of alcohol is simply down to him hearing voices and emptying the contents of his stomach onto his own lap after a pipe session.'

'But … but to speak so, is this not treason?'

'I won't deny it has put us in a treacherous position. To come out against the Chamberlain directly would draw the ire of the nobles, not just in the city but across the whole kingdom. To fully side with him, it would lose us our faithful. Especially as we know he is mad.'

Brother Jonns stared at the Abbott. Abbot Kayzen looked back and smiled.

'He will be the cause of his own demise, Brother, you mark my words,' Abbott Kayzen said, turning his attention back to tapping on the brickwork. 'He will, at some point soon, declare that the Gods have told him something like he can fly, in which case we will find him spread across the cobblestones beneath the citadel. Or he will try to declare himself the true High King, and I will leave it up to your imagination as to how the actual High King will respond.'

'I'm sorry, Abbott, but I still don't understand what we are doing here, in the catacombs?'

'Ah ha!' Abbott Kayzen cried out. He pushed on one of the old bricks in the wall. It gave way with a click, followed by a low rumble as a section of the wall, just bigger than a man was wide, began to open. 'What we need to do, Brother, is to keep those with influence on our side.'

'How do we do that?'

'With beer,' replied Abbott Kayzen as two monks rolled a barrel out of the secret door. 'With a lot of beer.'

DEAR MIKE

RAY OFFIAH

Dear Mike,

*Thank you very much for your critique on my latest piece
entitled 'For Whom the Orchids Bloom.'*
*Though I did find phrases such as, 'I got halfway through
and thought, "What's the point?"' less than helpful, I will
take on board your criticism that my writing 'lacks broad
appeal' and that 'I should write a vampire novel instead.'
You said that as we're such good friends, you felt sure I
would take your comments in the spirit in which they
were intended, and so to demonstrate that indeed there
are no hard feelings, I'm sending you the first chapter of
the suggested vampire novel.*

Enjoy.

MIKE, THE VAMPIRE WHO WAS DECIDEDLY AVERAGE IN BED

'IF YOU DON'T MIND me saying so …' Mike knows he has to tread carefully here, but if he's parting with this much cash then he also has to be very sure.

'What,' she says, with the velveteen charm of a Rottweiler. The woman sitting in the shadow of their corner booth is barely five feet tall. She looks like she's in her mid-fifties, though it's hard to tell since she's dressed in a loose-fitting Panda bear onesie, (complete with fluffy-eared hood), and a pair of large 'My Little Pony' slippers. What Mike can see of her face and neck is covered in a thick white paste and bright red lipstick that looks like it's been applied in the dark, with bandaged hands, while holding a spade.

She puts Mike in mind of Wee Jimmy Krankie, if Wee Jimmy Krankie had been fathered by Pennywise the Clown.

'Go on say it.' She takes a vaper out of her handbag. 'Everyone else does.'

'Well, I was just thinking …'

'Spit it out, you cockwomble.'

Charmed, I'm sure, Mike thinks. 'I was just thinking that you don't really look like a vampire.'

'Right,' she says, jamming the vaper between her lips.

Mike glances around. It's the middle of the day so the rest of the bar is empty. Still, vaping indoors …

'Tell me … Mike, is it?'

Mike nods.

'Tell me, Mike, know a lot of vampires, do you?'

Mike has to confess that she's the first vampire (allegedly) he's ever met.

'So it's fair to say that you don't know what a vampire's supposed to look like.'

He can't argue with the logic, and as if to punctuate her point, she takes a deep drag on her vaper then blows smoke from her nostrils, mouth – and two very tiny holes in her neck.

'If you tell me you can't meet at night because you work the late shift at a bakery, then a vampire in a onesie slathered in factor two-thousand sunscreen is what you're going to get.'

'I didn't know it went that high.'

'Not usually,' she says. 'This stuff would probably give me skin cancer,' she takes another drag, 'if I wasn't already dead. Right, I'm Doreen, pleased to meetcha.'

It's a firm handshake, though very cold.

'Okay, time's wasting, so down to business. You want me to turn you, yeah?'

Mike nods.

'Why?'

'Why do you care?'

She shrugs. 'I don't, but I also don't want you coming back complaining that you can't shave without a reflection, or blood doesn't taste as good as you heard it did, or you miss taking a shit.'

Mike doesn't think he'll particularly miss taking a shit.

'So let me guess: it's the sex, isn't it?'

'No, it isn't,' Mike says, looking down forlornly into his Tight Snatch[1].

'Been watching *True Blood?* Wanna go at the missus like a pneumatic drill?' Doreen raps her knuckles on the table, almost a hundred taps in a second by Mike's wide-eyed reckoning.

'It's not like that,' he says, staring at the smouldering hole in Doreen's side of the table. 'I just want to make her happy.'

'Right, right. Lacking in the stamina department?'

'No, I'm not lacking in the—'

'Ah, it's a size thing then?'

'No, it's—'

'A Bit like throwing a chipolata into the Grand Canyon?'

'No! It fucking isn't!'

'All right, all right, calm your trousers!'

'Look, Doreen, I want to be a vampire because I want more time to get better at things! And no, not just the sex! I want to learn how to play the saxophone. I want to learn how to fly a plane.'

'At night?'

'Cook gourmet meals! Climb the Matterhorn! Bake better Victoria Sponges!'

'Also at night.'

'I want to learn how to appreciate good literature so when friends ask me to critique their writing, I can make a meaningful assessment of their work!'

Doreen nods appreciatively. 'That sounds very noble.'

'So, will you do it?'

'A thousand deposit, up front,' Doreen says, leaning back in her chair. 'Meet me at Caversham Cemetery at midnight. It's private and I rent a plot there for this kind of thing.'

Mike is about to point out he has a shift at the bakery, then thinks better of it.

'We do the business. I bury you, dig you up three days later, and Bob's your undead uncle.' It's clearly her favourite line; she grins expectantly at him. He can see one of her fangs is missing.

'Rest of the hundred grand I can take in instalments.'

'One hundred grand!' Mike screeches, almost falling off his chair.

'In instalments,' she reminds him.

'It'll take years to pay that off!'

'You'll be immortal, you prick; what does it matter?'

Again, she has a point.

'Okay, tonight then,' he agrees. 'Caversham Cemetery.'

'You know it makes sense,' Doreen says. She takes one more drag on her vaper, and when she exhales, their corner of the bar fills instantly with smoke that smells like a Big Mac Meal fried in despair.

The smoke begins to clear, and Doreen has disappeared.

At first, Mike is astonished, then slightly less so when he turns in his seat and sees a small fat panda hurrying towards the exit.

---

1. One shot of vodka, one shot of peach schnapps, orange juice, cranberry juice

THE NIGHTWATCHMAN

JULIE ROBERTS

CHARLIE JACKSON WALKED between the stacked barrels in the brewery yard towards the single wooden door at the end of the red bricked wall. He put his canvas bag on the ground and breathed in deeply. The daylight was shortening now, and it would still be dark when he came out tomorrow.

It took five minutes to reach his eight-foot square cubby-hole that management called an office. But over the years he had made it his own cosy space, with a fireside chair he'd picked up at the Woman's Institute jumble sale, a round table that Mrs Willoughby was throwing out for firewood and a single gas ring from Bill Smith, his next-door neighbour. It had cost him a packet of Woodbine ciggies, but a nice cup of tea at three o'clock helped to keep him awake. The electric two bar fire had been installed with the generosity of the foreman, and only then because he had found Charlie wearing his over-coat covered with frost one morning last winter.

Charlie hung his jacket and bag on the brass hook. He flicked the switch and the overhead bulb glowed down over his desk. His last bit of comfort was the well-padded seat of a dining room chair. He patted his trouser pocket and pulled out a packet of Players, his one luxury in this life of rationing, blackout and everlasting news of the war, London bombings and death. What he watched on the Pathé News at the Odeon was worse than the Great War.

He checked the clipboard for messages – none tonight, all ship shape and quiet. He pulled a notebook and pencil from his bag. Sitting on the chair he ran his finger over the cover and the black inked title: *Charlie Jackson's Journal.*

He flicked through the sheets until he came to a blank page.

Licking the tip of his pencil he wrote:

23rd August 1943.

This is a special shift tonight. I have been the night watchman here in Simonds Brewery for the past twenty years. Five years after I was demobbed from the army in 1918. Tried my hand at being a milkman, but the old mare, Daisy, needed a lot of care after I finished clinking the bottles on the doorsteps. I changed jobs to being a coalman; that was worse. It was easy enough at the terrace houses with openings down into the cellar. It was the terraces with front gardens that were tricky - I had to carry them sacks along the hall passage, through the living room and out the back door to the coal shed with the missus laying down newspaper for me boots and telling me to mind the furniture.

When this job at the brewery came up, I jumped at it. Eight hours working while the rest of the town is asleep. And the job is just that, watching, listening, getting me exercise walking around the vats that are fermenting and making a good pint of best ale. It has also given me time to think over me life, because you never know when it might come to an end.

I was one of eighteen children, although there was only nine of us at the end of Ma's life, four boys and five girls. Three of us boys were old enough to go in the army. The years don't fade the horrors of living in the trenches, the bombardments from dawn till dusk and sweating with fear of a German bullet when the whistle went to go over the top. I came home; Willy did too, but he has never been the same. He dreams, and Dotty holds him tight and rocks him back to sleep. Johnny never made it. He was the oldest son and died at the Somme.

Enough of doom and gloom. We had a happy house, a two up, three down terrace built of good solid bricks, slate roof and a fire-place in each room. On cold mornings Ma would light the gas oven and leave the door open when we washed our faces, arms and under our armpits, something she always insisted on and I quote, 'There's nothing worse than a smelly man.'

The only place I could find to read my books in peace was the outside privy. This was fine, but in winter, nah, I put bits of rag in my ears and sat in the corner under the window in the kitchen. Some of the neighbours, who thought they were one step above us in the pecking line of society, called it their living room. We had crammed in a sideboard, table, six stools and two armchairs, one for Ma to knit and darn our socks and Pa to read every page of the daily newspaper. The door down to the spooky cellar had a high bolt, so we youngsters couldn't reach it and fall down the well-trodden steps to the bottom. The gas and electric meters were fixed on the wall, but in winter when we had a fire, Ma or Pa would go down for a bucket of coal. Only when I was ten did I get asked to 'go and fetch a bucket of coal, Charlie.'

The front room was only used on special occasions, but always *at Christmas. In there was the sofa, and the piano, that my sister, Mable, loved to play all the modern tunes on. The potted aspidistra in front of the window was Ma's symbol of respectability.*

Suddenly a shrill ring stopped Charlie writing. He put his pencil and notebook back in his bag.

'I'm on my way,' he called out, picking up a bunch of keys and going out into the cavernous brewery room. Reaching the outside door, he unlocked and opened it.

'On time as usual Dotty. And who do we have here?'

The little girl holding Dotty's hand laughed. 'Uncle Charlie, you know me, I'm Wendy.' She held out a paper bag. 'I've got a slice of fruit cake for you, but there aren't many currants in it.'

'Did mummy bake it?'

'Yes, and I cut the slice for you, just a bit bigger than mine.'

'Come on then, let's get back to my cubby-hole. We can have a nice cup of tea.'

Wendy ran forward and Charlie lifted her into his arms. 'I'll carry you in. Is that OK?'

She nodded.

Dotty walked beside Charlie holding a pudding basin in her hands. 'This is a creepy place to spend your working life. It's a good job you're not married; no sensible woman would put up with you not being in the bed most nights of the year.'

Charlie looked at her and winked. 'But there are always the afternoons.'

When they reached Charlie's room Dotty put the basin on the desk. 'It's another meatless stew, but I've managed a healthy selection of veg.'

'Whatever, sis, it's good of you to bring something each week. It beats jam sandwiches.'

He took three enamel mugs off a shelf and filled them with tea from a flask.

Wendy torn open the paper bag. 'Our cake, Uncle Charlie.'

'That looks delicious. You can sit with me in the armchair and mummy at the desk.'

They ate their cake and sipped the tea.

Dotty picked up last week's washed basin. 'As always, a short visit, Charlie, enjoy your supper.'

Wendy squeezed one of Charlie's fingers. 'Will the big rats be coming out now?'

'No. They only come out after midnight. They know you don't like them.' Charlie picked her up. 'I'll carry you and if you see one, shout, and we'll chase it away.'

Charlie flicked a switch and light filled the outer room. With a sprightly step he set off back to the outside door.

'See you next week.'

'Thanks Dotty, 'bye Wendy.'

Charlie locked the door and turned. The vats cast deep shadow along the walkways, the smell of the beer stronger each evening. Seeing Dotty out he used as his outward patrol; going back he zig-zagged, checking the furthest vats and the corners for those rats that frightened Wendy.

Charlie stopped. A noise was coming from near his room. The sound was … a meow and then another. He crept forward and there, lying on the concrete floor was a cat with four kittens.

'Well, well, Mrs Tabby, what have we here?' He knelt and

stroked the cat's head between her ears. 'I think you had best come with me. I'll just fetch me bag.'

Ten minutes later, Mrs Tabby was laying on his woollen pullover with her kittens snuggled close.

Charlie sat at his desk and opened his notebook and licked the pencil lead.

He wrote:

I found Mrs Tabby and family tonight. I'm going to keep her; someone to talk to. When the weather changes for the worst we can sit together, she'll be my hot water bottle. And I'm sure Dotty will find good homes for her kittens.

And tonight, has certainly been an anniversary to remember.

BISCUIT MAN

ANDY BENNETT

LIONEL FELT a tug on the rear of his outfit. Of course, he did. It was relentless as a junior sales representative, better known as the current wearer of Biscuit Man's foam outfit. Large round biscuit on the front, same at the rear, and him, the large cream filling in the middle, all dressed in white spandex.

He turned and looked down. A boy looked back up, and some feet away, his mother, camera in hand.

'Can I get a picture, Biscuit Man?'

Lionel knew his duty in the situation. He puffed up his chest, and replied in the most bellowing tone he could: Sure thing, kiddo. It's Biscuit Man's pleasure. What's your name?'

'Mark.'

'And what brings you here, Mark? A calamity in the centre of town?'

'No,' replied the boy awkwardly.

'A desperate disaster in deepest downtown?'

'No.'

'An ecological emergency on the edge of the city?'

'No.'

'What then kid?'

'A photo.'

Lionel didn't want to seem perturbed, but these kids should know how to take part.

He grabbed for his dough ball cannon – a large plastic drainpipe with a handle and a ball of doughy looking material poking out of the end.

'Okay. Pose, kid. And think crime fighting thoughts.'

They stood together while the boy's mother took a couple of photos.

Lionel reached down to the gift box and pulled out a promotional comic and a bag of dough ball cannonballs – delicious but slightly gooey on the teeth.

'Here you go, Mark, have some treats, and be law abiding!'

'Sure thing, Biscuit Man, and I have something for you—'

This was something new, the kids normally just wanted free stuff.

The boy held out his hand inverted. Lionel put his hand beneath to catch this mysterious item. The boy looked up.

'You are our last hope. I have faith in you, you've just got to believe,' he said, the words no longer seeming to belong to a small child, but instead echoing deeply round Lionel's head. The boy held nothing but instead grabbed Lionel's hand. The boy's fingers seemed to be made of pure lightning such was the pain. There was nothing for it, but to pass out.

Lionel awoke and opened his eyes. Kitty of Media Relations was standing above him.

'I leave you alone for a minute and you end up having a snooze on the pavement.'

'Did you see that kid, just now? Little runt played some prank.'

'Nope, haven't seen anyone; would've seen them through the store window. No one ever comes this near to closing time.'

Lionel didn't know how to answer, maybe he had imagined it – the last bit certainly made no sense. He stood up, even if it was a trick of the mind, he still felt really pained from something.

'Come on, Mr Biscuit, we can go home now.'

The new day dawned. The sun was shining through the window, and casting a bright pattern on the bed covers. Lionel breathed deeply, and felt energised. He thought back to the encounter from the day before and gave his hand a squeeze. Nothing, no pain to speak of, if anything he had never felt so healthy. The normal array of morning aches and pains seemed to be gone for once.

He got up. Something else was clear now. He was dressed as Biscuit Man – massive biscuit front and back. He didn't understand as he definitely had taken the costume off the day before. He went to look in the mirror. His makeup was immaculate, and his hair, not a strand out of place. He felt confused, but also pride in his appearance. Somewhere deep down, however, a nagging sense of nervous tension was building. Despite the apparent joys of the day, he knew a deep menace lurked.

He heard a cry from the window, and ran over to hear better.

'Help … Help, we can't get out.' The voice was distant but distinct.

The city's high-rise blocks stretched out in straight lines in both directions to left and right. Traffic proceeded slowly as always interrupted by impatient horn blasts, and people jostled on the pavements for their right to get to their activities for the day. He looked to see what the voice might be. Nothing was clear amongst the melee of normality, but, then, the voice again.

'Help!'

He spun his head to the left, now acutely aware of the direction. In the far distance there were flames climbing the side of a tower block. He focused in, and there at one of the windows, was a woman. He didn't know how, but even at such a distance her words were clear and her every movement stood out. Fire fighters were trying, but the heat was too intense.

Without a further thought, he thrust the window open, and jumped out.

Lionel looked at the pavement rapidly approaching, and had to wonder. From a six-story apartment, jumping out might have been a poor choice. However, he landed expertly – his legs just seeming extra rubbery and shock absorbing, almost a little doughy.

There was no time to waste, averting a tragedy awaited. He bounded in the direction of the cries, each rubbery leap taking metres off the distance. The slow-moving city traffic was no match for his pace as he bounded expertly over obstacles and through gaps in search of the most efficient route. He reached the building and ran straight for the door.

The heat was intense. He listened. There were faint cries from higher in the building. He dashed for the stairs and began to bound floor by floor. It was an inferno, and he could smell hints of burnt biscuit coming from his protective suit.

He burst through the stairwell door. The whole floor was filling with smoke. He focused his senses, listening for the slightest sound and looking for heat traces. A woman, a girl and a dog were all at the far end apartment.

He smashed the door, walked in and surveyed the room. The people were cowering towards the back.

He turned, and without thought, raised his hand. A white doughy slurry spewed from its general direction. It looked gross, and Lionel felt sick, but it was filling the doorway and blocking the heat nicely.

Lionel approached and boomed, 'Don't worry, Biscuit Man's here. And who's this cute puppy?'

'Oh, Biscuit Man. I knew you'd save us. He's, Danny,' replied the girl.

'We'll have you and Danny out in jiffy—', he patted the dog, '—And now, to escape.'

He ran to the window. Flung it open and thrust his hand out. White dough began to pour again. It wasn't random, in Lionel's mind there was an image of a tubular escape chute, and under his control it was forming that shape.

'Make your way out.'

One by one, they slid to safety.

The girl turned to Lionel, 'Thank you, Biscuit Man, and Danny thanks you too.' The dog barked in agreement.

Tragedy averted, and a warm feeling of success. For once, he had done something good. One last look around, before jumping himself to join the glory outside.

The chute was a smooth tube curving towards flat for a slow safe landing. Or so Lionel expected, but his trip was cut short by a collision with a solid obstruction. It was pitch black and disorienting, but for just moments. A mighty crash followed as the biscuit tube smashed into pieces with him inside. He began trying to orient himself compared to the buildings as he flew sideways, but something smashed into his back propelling him faster and unstoppably into the side of a truck.

Winded, he fell to the ground.

'Thought you could stop me, Biscuit Man.'

The smell of freshly baked bread filled the air. This could only mean one thing. He climbed to his feet and faced his foe, just metres away, floating on a yeasty exhaust.

'The Bread Baron …' Lionel felt balls of dough forming in his hands in readiness.

'Indeed, I knew you would come the moment you heard a cry of distress. You imprisoned me last time, but now I'm back to deal with you properly.'

Lionel wasn't so convinced he'd met the Bread Baron other than via the advertising comic. He felt being smacked about by someone dressed like a wholemeal bloomer might be more memorable. Something deep down confirmed that for Biscuit Man this wasn't the first time.

Lionel didn't wait, and threw a dough ball. A direct hit – mid chest. The Baron hardly moved. Lionel threw the second. Still not much movement.

'Is that all you've got.' The Baron pulled a crusty loaf from seemingly nowhere and threw it. Lionel managed to dodge it before it smashed a hole into the side of the truck. He ducked under the vehicle and started to run towards the cover of nearby buildings just in time to avoid a barrage of loaves that decimated cars and shop fronts behind him.

He ran around a corner into a back street and wondered how to deal with this. Two more balls of hard dough were forming in his hands. He threw one at a wall – almost no impact, but then a loaf followed it up smashing a hole. He ran further, looking for a place to hide, but a loaf smashed into his back pinning him to the pavement and creating a Biscuit Man shaped imprint.

He rolled over to see the Baron above, forming a large loaf between his arms and raising it ready to throw.

Lionel closed his eyes. He couldn't cope with looking.

Deep in his head, words began circling, 'You are our last hope … I have faith in you … You've just got to believe …' They were Mark's from earlier

Lionel knew he had to try, and somehow that allowed him to find some confidence. He opened his eyes, looked at the balls of dough in his hands and believed they could move. They flew from his hands without him even trying this time, and smashed into the Baron throwing him and his massive loaf into the building behind.

Lionel stood, his limbs hurt from the impact, but that mattered less now, and two more ball of dough were forming in his hands.

The Baron emerged from the building. He looked angrier than ever, and didn't hesitate in launching the next attack. The loaf onslaught was brutal, but Lionel found himself able to dodge and deflect them with dough balls.

The two stood, evenly matched, pounding at each other.

'That's the Biscuit Man I remember! Much better,' said the Baron, 'but still not good enough; you care too much.' He breathed out a cloud of flour enveloping himself. It ignited in a bright flame, and he vanished.

Lionel surveyed the carnage of the road, and felt sad. They'd caused so much damage. At least the people had had the sense to run and hide. He sighed and began walking away.

He was soon interrupted by the sound of screams. It could only mean one thing. He took in a deep breath and savoured one last moment of peace, and then began running towards the sound.

He was greeted by the sight of a spinning tornado of cars in the middle of an intersection with the Bread Baron spinning and blowing at the bottom.

'Stop this,' Lionel screamed.

'Okay,' replied the Baron, 'if I must.'

The cars began to tumble from the sky. Lionel put his arms up and sprayed doughy cushions under each.

'I told you; you care too much. What a lot of wasted effort. You could've taken me then, but these people matter too much to you.'

The Bread Baron floated down to the ground. The two stood facing each other in duelling position.

'Puny human … you were no match for my loaves… now taste my full wrath.'

The Baron breathed in, raised his hands. Lionel knew Biscuit Man had something brewing too. He could feel it rising up his throat. He drew in, then they unleashed at the same time.

Yeast wind against biscuit breath, the two blew with all their might. One pushing first and then the other. Where the two forces met a powerful wind blew sideways moving parked cars, pushing trees to their limits and smashing glass in buildings.

Biscuit Man focused, he couldn't let the Baron be left undefeated, and blew all he could. He began walking in against the massive force, but there was a scream to his left. The airflow was making a shop window flex and bow. It had been a safe refuge, but Lionel saw the occupants terrified faces and knew he had to withdraw to save them. A yeasty onslaught took over and rammed him hard against the ground, shortly followed by layers of quickly hardening bread dough.

From inside his bread tomb, Lionel heard the Baron's voice, 'Your hero is gone, people, his love of you is his weakness. Biscuits are no more. Make way for bread.'

Lionel lay encased and motionless. He knew Biscuit Man's metabolism reduced his need for air, but it wouldn't last forever, and his consciousness was drifting away.

'Biscuit Man wouldn't give up,' Lionel thought to himself, 'He is fearless and resourceful.' However, Lionel just wished he could return to the day before and being a pretend super hero.

Lionel thought, 'There must be something, Biscuit Man is

supposed to be invincible. And here's me, regular guy, just with some fancy spandex.'

He began to despair, but, 'Of course, the suit… the power in the suit.'

Lionel remembered in one of the comics, Biscuit Man had used the suit's power against the Baron. The outcome hadn't been good for either of them, but it seemed worth a shot. He focused his mind.

Initially there was nothing, but the more he thought the hotter the suit became. He could sense the danger as the power became increasingly more overloaded inside the biscuit panels. The pain from the burning heat was becoming more than his will power could deal with, but he needed to do this. He focused once more, and the intensity rose exponentially and detonation occurred. The bread dough was no match. It flew apart and Lionel found himself airborne.

Without the biscuit panels he was more agile than before. He landed nimbly, and began running towards the Bread Baron who had taken fun in smashing more of the city.

'You stop that! Biscuit Man says no!'

He ran at the Baron, fists out. The Baron flew back landing hard.

He crawled up, 'So, you escaped from my bread, fine job, but you are still weak, and there is much more where that came from.'

The Baron breathed in ready to unleash with all his force, but Biscuit Man was ready this time. The dough balls were already in his hands and he willed them away with unstoppable intensity. They smashed into the Baron's face so rapidly he had no chance to respond. Then more and more. Like a machine gun of dough balls in each hand, the onslaught was relentless. Soon all that stood in front of Lionel was a large mound of slowly solidifying biscuit dough.

He walked up to the pile and battered it aside. The Baron wasn't moving, but he was breathing. Biscuit Man formed some biscuit restraints to prevent his escape, and then left him to the police to deal with.

He turned to the onlookers, and said, 'You are free now, the Baron is gone.'

Biscuit Man sat down on the pavement, he felt exhausted.

A small child approached. It was Mark. 'Thanks, Lionel. I knew you could do it.'

AN UNCERTAIN HUNGER

JILLIAN BOST

I'VE EATEN six custard creams, the last of the pack, and yet I find myself rummaging through Mum's purse, hoping she won't notice when I snag a pound so I can sneak off to the corner shop and buy more. If I eat enough of the new pack until there are six left, then throw away the other wrapper in someone else's bin, she won't even know I've had any.

I'm in luck when Mum calls out that she's about to take a shower. She always takes ages. I tell her I'll just be watching telly. I wait two minutes, then open and close the front door, quiet as a mouse. I dart off to the shop and come back with the biscuits and a penny to spare.

I've crammed down almost half the pack when part of the biscuit gets stuck in my throat and I start to cough. Tears stream down my cheeks and my heart thumps with panic. I fill this morning's tea mug with tap water and try to drink it down, but I spit it back up.

Fuck. I'm dying. I'm dying and it's all my fault for being such a pathetic pig.

'Emma!' Mum rushes into the kitchen, her dressing gown

hastily wrapped around her and her hair dripping wet. She pounds me on the back and the biscuit finally dislodges itself. I swallow it, though it feels like I'm thanking a bully for hitting me in the stomach.

'Jesus, Em. Are you all right?' Mum grips my shoulders and peers at me, as if my red eyes and wet cheeks will give her an NHS-level diagnosis.

'Yeah,' I rasp. 'Just—went down the wrong pipe I guess. Thanks. You saved me.' I try to smile.

She tuts. 'Be more careful. You don't need to wolf those things down like there's no tomorrow.'

My face burns. 'I know. I'll try to remember to chew next time.'

As she goes off to dry her hair, I realise she didn't clock that it was a new pack of custard creams. She thinks I was just having one or two biscuits like a sane person, like someone who doesn't ram food down their throat until their stomach aches.

It's not quite the victory I'd hoped it would be.

'Emma? You all right, darlin?'

I wipe my dripping nose with a bit of toilet paper. 'Yeah,' I call, and cringe. My voice is shaky.

When I open the door, my dad has disappeared, but as I enter the living room, he gets up from the sofa. 'Emma! I knew something was wrong.'

Guess I wasn't as good at hiding my sobs as I thought. 'It's nothing. I just, uh, got dirt in my eye.'

He frowns. 'And why's your hair all wet?'

'I just … my eye was bothering me so much I thought I'd better rinse it out.'

Dad stares at me for a moment, then sighs. 'Fine, have it your way.'

My stomach roils. What does he want me to say? *Oh yeah, it's fine, just some local kids who called me a fat cunt and threw an egg at me that nailed me right in the back of the head so I had to run back here to wash it out. No big deal.*

His nose wrinkles. 'Do you smell egg?'

'Wha—I don't know. Didn't you make eggs for breakfast?'

'Oh. Yes, I did. Huh. Guess I'm losing me mind in me old age.'

I force a chuckle. 'Come off it, Dad, you're only forty-three.'

'But I don't look a day over thirty.' We laugh together even though it isn't that funny, and he puts the footy on, and I go to my room and inhale a few of my secret chocolate digestives. I make sure to brush my teeth after, since my dad apparently has such a sensitive nose now.

When Mum picks me up from Dad's place, she surprises me with a Big Mac and fries. I can't remember ever not being happy about surprise McDonald's before.

'Mum?' I ask once we're inside watching *Family Fortunes*. 'Do you think you could make a salad for tea tomorrow?'

She stares at me. 'Salad? You hate salad. Unless it's covered in salad cream, maybe.'

Wow. Low blow. 'I know, but I'm … I think it might be good to eat healthier, yeah? Like I know I eat a lot of, well, fast food and biscuits, like.'

Mum hmms, then says, 'Well you'll need something more

filling than salad, but I'll try to make something healthy for us, all right?'

'Yeah, cool. Cheers Mum.'

The next night, she presents me with a veg lasagne. It smells great, tastes better, but it's got loads of cheese. Three kinds: ricotta, cheddar, and mozzarella. I look up the calories on my phone; can't even find an estimate, but I know it must be a lot.

'Is that better, love?' Mum caresses my hair after I've finished my tea. 'Do you want seconds?'

'No.' I push my plate away. 'It's actually—I mean it tasted good, but it's still pretty fattening, you know?'

Mum's lips tighten into a thin line. 'If you have a problem with what I cook, you can fix your own meals, young lady.'

I stand up, and my chair jerks back against the floor with a screech. 'Do you want me to be fat all my life? Is that it? You want a fat daughter? So then you can feel okay about being fat yourself?'

Mum rears back, then gets to her feet. 'Get up to your room before I smack you. I'm dead serious, Emma. You can't talk to me like that.'

I start to speak, but the cold glare of my mother makes my insides churn. I hurry upstairs.

'I'd better not see you in this kitchen the rest of the night if you're so worried about food!' Mum calls after me.

My eyes burn with unshed tears. I want to smash the mirrors, I want to tear up the duvets. She wants me to fail. I won't do it. I'm not going to be a gross fat pig anymore.

Even as this new determination courses through my blood, I long to go to the back of my wardrobe and demolish the Oreos I have hidden on the top shelf.

Instead, I force myself to just lie on the bed and take slow, deep breaths. I can feel my belly oozing out over my jeans. I squeeze the flab, gently at first, then harder. 'You're disgusting,' I murmur. 'Learn some self-control.'

There's a soft knock at my door, and I gasp. Did she hear me?

'Emma? Can I come in?'

I want to tell her to fuck off, but instead I say 'Yeah, all right.'

She enters my room, and sits down on the edge of the bed. She touches my ankle. 'Look, I'm sorry, okay? I think neither of us is going about this the right way, but we do need to eat better. You are right about that. We should work together on this. Not with shouting matches. How about we do the shopping together this weekend and we can work on making some healthy meals and snacks. Sound good?'

I sit up. 'Yeah. Thanks, Mum.'

''Course, darling.' She wraps her arms around me and squeezes me tight. I hug her back, and think maybe we've solved it. If we're in this together, I'm less likely to fail.

After school the next day, I get pushed down into the mud, and the Year 11 boys roar with laughter. At least they don't try to stop me from getting away. I wipe off as much mud as I can, and head to the nearest corner shop to buy some shortbread.

I regret it before I've even left the store. I almost put the biscuits back on the counter, but instead I stuff them inside my tote bag and dart away.

My stomach is roiling as if I've committed a crime. My blood darts around like it's lost its way.

Seated outside the Lloyds a little way down the road is a homeless man, covered in a blanket and reading a book.

I dig the biscuits out of my bag, and with a fluttering pulse, I go up to the man and clear my throat. I hold out the biscuits like a peace offering. 'Excuse me? Um, would you like these?'

The guy eyes me and my mud-splattered clothes but takes the package of shortbread from my shaking hand. 'Thanks,' he mutters.

'You're welcome.'

As I walk away, I gradually feel lighter. I'm not sure this is even a victory. But there is hope.

I've given myself that, at least.

ANTS

FRANCES BRINDLE

'GOOD MORNING, you've reached Lorraine at Humpty and Balmers, how can I help you?'

'Are you the company that makes the biscuits?'

'We are indeed sir; biscuits are our business.'

'It's just that I've had an idea.'

'Wonderful, we love hearing what our customers think. Can you tell me what your idea is, sir?'

'It's an idea for a biscuit. It's like two chocolate biscuits sandwiched together with a chocolate filling.'

'Like a Bourbon?'

'What's a Bourbon?'

'It's very similar to the biscuit you've just described, sir. If you give me your address, I'll send you a voucher and you can try one for yourself. They're very nice, I often have one with my coffee.'

'What about two biscuits, with a custard flavour cream in the middle?'

'That's a custard cream. We make those too sir.'

'A plain round biscuit you can dunk in your tea?'

'A rich tea biscuit.'

'Does that mean I won't get paid for my ideas?'

'I'm afraid not.'

'I have more ideas.'

'OK.'

'What about a biscuit made with ants.'

'Ants?'

'Yes, you know how you can get chocolate-covered ants, well this is an ant biscuit. I bet you don't have anything like that, do you?'

'No sir, you're right, we don't.'

'It doesn't have to be ants, you could use any insect, like spiders, or flies, or even ladybirds if you wanted to add a bit of colour. And wasps, there are always plenty of wasps around in the summer.'

'I'm not sure our customers would want to eat insects, sir.'

'Really? I can't imagine why not, I eat insects all the time they're very tasty and high in protein, I'm chewing on a grasshopper now. Look, why don't I send you a sample and you can pass it on to the people who make the biscuits.'

'A sample of grasshoppers?'

'No of course not, ants. Grasshoppers taste like chicken - you wouldn't want a biscuit that tasted like chicken now, would you?'

'I suppose not.'

'Perfect, well that's settled, I'll send you a box of ants and you can transfer the money for the idea into my account when you get it. I have to say after a slow start, it's been a pleasure dealing with you, Lorraine.'

'Thank you, sir, it's been a pleasure talking to you too. Is there anything else I can help you with?'

'No, I think I'm good.'

'Excellent. Goodbye, then sir.'

'Goodbye, Lorraine. Enjoy the ants.'

HUNTLEY'S MONSTER

RAY OFFIAH

November 3rd 1856

THOUGH THE EVENTS I will attempt to chronicle occurred more than a year ago, it is only now that my nerves are sufficiently recovered I can put pen to paper.

My good wife tells me I have not uttered ten words since that fateful night.

I do not know.

I cannot remember.

I do know that I have not left the sanctity of my home since I was found wandering the streets of Cemetery Junction, uttering profanities against man and God.

No, I will not set foot outside my home – for now I know the depravity that festers in the minds of men.

I am George Palmer: a quaker, businessman, and joint proprietor of *Huntley & Palmer,* a company of biscuit makers that, since its modest beginnings, has made its home in the industrious and god-fearing town of Reading, an otherwise unremarkable industrial nexus nestled in the Borough of Royal Berkshire.

The company was founded as *J. Huntley & Son,* and enjoyed small success in the locality of the South, eking moderate profits selling its wares to the well-healed denizens of Maidenhead and London.

Joseph Huntley, the founder, suffered ill-health in his later years, and so handed the business to his eldest son, Thomas; and though Thomas, a diligent, devout man, possessed a flamboyant, almost foppish flair in the design and production of hard-baked consumable products, the Good Lord had chosen not to endow him with a similar interest or acumen for strategy. However, what Thomas lacked in business skills, he more than made up for in pragmatism: he was a man who recognised his own shortcomings, a trait so rare in many of us these days.

And so he came to me, an old friend from the church, and asked if I would be his partner. He would continue to indulge his passion for experimentation, and the world's strange new predilection for covering shortbread in chocolate, while I would handle the day-to-day running of the factory, and the plans for our expansion.

We changed the name of the company to cement our alliance, and it prospered under our joint leadership. We expanded to the four corners of the British Isles, delivering the finest assortment of biscuits from Stornaway to Lizard's Point.

And we looked further.

The continent beckoned, and after that, the Americas.

I remember that after a delicious repast prepared by his good wife, we sat in front of the fire. Conversation turned to business, so the women adjourned to the rear parlour. It was a cold night, but our spirits were lifted by a plate of shortbreads and the fine scotch Thomas had been saving for a special occasion.

'And what is this occasion, Thomas?' I asked.

He simply smiled and settled back into his chair, his eyes closed and a look of serenity played across his features. 'It is simply a feeling of completeness, my friend. You, me, the factory ... Just you wait and see. We will own the world.'

Looking back to that night of contentment, I think on my own negligence: how my ambition blinded me to the changes in Thomas that took hold of him so soon after. The reasons for Thomas's descent, my own complicity in his downfall – they matter not; what matters is that over the next few years I failed to pay heed to how restless he became. His inventive nature sat ill at ease with our continuing success. In some ways he longed for our earlier days of adventure and uncertainty, our struggles to be accepted as learned fellows of biscuit production.

Thomas began to look upon our fine work with despair.

'Look at the floor, George!' he would cry. 'The waste!'

The sight of broken biscuits, spilt chocolate and discarded fondants drove him to a state of apoplexy. The factory girls became wary of him, perhaps frightened; and yet, inebriated with our conquest of France and Spain, I dismissed their concerns without a second thought.

That is until Molly came to me one day.

She was a stout creature of nineteen years, and yet, strangely, unmarried; perhaps because she was often given to day-dreaming and flights of fancy, believing that one day she would gain an education and serve as a member of parliament, or as an ambassador to the Americas. Such nonsense!

But I have fallen to distraction. Forgive me.

Molly came to me and said that as she cleaned the floors that previous evening she had witnessed Thomas engaged in the strangest of activities: he was sweeping up the remains from the factory machinery and gathering vats of discarded icing and sugar. Then he loaded them upon a trolley and wheeled it down to his laboratories in the basement. She followed him in secret but dared not enter his chambers. (As is right and proper: how a man conducts himself within his own private chambers is best beyond the ken of womenfolk.)

'There is evil at play there, Mr Palmer,' she said. 'You mark my words.'

I told her, kindly, that she was prattling like an ageing spinster and that if she had put her mind to improving her baking instead of scrutinising the comings and goings of her betters, then perhaps she would not have found herself without a husband so far into her child-bearing years. To my astonishment, she helped herself to one of my biscuits, scribbled out a barely legible resignation on the wrapper, and threw it at me, accompanied by a litany of expletives that would have made a drayman blush. And then she left, without closing the door. Surely raised by wolves, or the Welsh …

Over the coming weeks, Thomas's ramblings ('Waste! Waste! Such terrible waste!') grew more and more feverish. I began to wonder if there was some truth in what that shrew of a woman had said. My suspicions were aroused further by unexplained items that had begun to appear on our supply invoices: pulleys and motorised winches, lightning rods, power transformers, electrical storage capacitors … Production was increasing, but there was no need for this equipment, not as far as I could ascertain. I was now certain that Molly had been correct all along: something sinister indeed was afoot in the basement of our factory.

And so, breaking all gentlemanly bonds of fellowship and trust, I hid myself behind one of the mixing vats until the late hours, and waited.

Sure enough, Thomas appeared and began gathering discarded biscuits, crumbs, sugar, fondant icing, and pieces of chocolate left on the conveyers. He gesticulated wildly, talking to himself as he picked scraps and flotsam from the churning machines and the ovens, loaded them upon his trolley and wheeled them to his basement sanctum.

I followed, in mind to keep myself from being seen; there was a strangeness about him; a demonic madness if you will, and I did fear that such insanity may be infectious.

I listened at the door of his lab, and heard the metallic grind of ungodly machinery, tasted the coppery taint of enormous electrical power, felt my soul chilled by the breath of the devil hard at his labours.

But I was, and remain, a devout man, so it is my sworn duty to save a fellow human being whose own soul is in peril, especially one who is … was … my lifelong friend.

So, with only my faith as my shield, I burst into the lab, and was greeted with a sight that shall haunt me for all my days.

Thomas stood, perspiring like a man possessed, amidst an array of panels, dials and switches. Electrical cables fed into a huge metal table in the centre of his lab; the surface of the table itself made up of a complex latticework of heating elements.

But it was the abomination lying upon it that froze me to my very marrow.

Made from the remains of broken shortbread, bourbon biscuits and whatever other remnants he found to hand – all bound together with stitches of candy floss and icing glue …

It was, and forever will be, the most enormous, most hideous gingerbread man I had ever seen: a gargantuan, grotesque affront to the noble art of baked confectionary.

'Thomas!' I cried. 'For the love of God, man; what have you done!'

He reached for the brass lever above his head with a feverish hand. 'For glory, George!' he shouted. 'For the glory of biscuit-making, now and ever more!'

And to my horror, he threw the lever.

I watched, struck mute, as the ceiling opened and the atrocity he had created was doused in a pungently rounded molten icing.

'Thomas! No!'

'Yes,' he screamed, 'a thousand times, yes!'

And God forgive me, I turned away. I turned from my friend and I ran, for what was I, a mere man … How could I hope to stand against such … evil, such base villainy, such insanity?

For my friend had committed the most heinous of sins: a ginger base coated with a vanilla and almond glaze? The after-taste alone would be blasphemy to the palate of the Good Lord himself.

It was then I knew, you see, that Thomas, my friend, was lost to me …

But now I am spent, good sir; the horrors I have witnessed have left me less than I was. I fear I can hold my pen no longer …

LOCKDOWN MELTDOWN

ILARIA WARREN

WE KNEW lockdown had got to us when Blanket turned four.

That day, our daughter dropped the bombshell on us and the news was initially met with 'yeah, right.' But then she said Blanket itself had told her, so we had to accept that new piece of information as true.

Nobody asked why Blanket's previous three birthdays hadn't been celebrated, or why this one was different. Could it be that blankets aged faster than human beings? Could this be one of its milestones? And worst of all, why were we discussing the development of an inanimate object?

Alas, the news was deemed as genuine, so we put together a Birthday Board and gathered around the coffee table. The first decision was to never mention the fact that Blanket was in fact six. It was a gift we'd received when our six-year-old daughter was born, and as they say down my neck of the woods, 'Maths is not an opinion.' Numbers don't lie.

As you know, time stopped during quarantine. Days all blurred into one, let alone the memory of past years. Calendars hadn't been used in months; so somehow, we shaved a couple of years off Blanket's age and cracked on with party preparations.

Conveniently, one of the Senior Members of the Birthday Board (which we will refer to as 'mummy' or 'yours truly') had finally learnt to bake. Between chocolate cookies, shortbreads and Italian biscuits, it was like Huntley and Palmers had exploded in this house. Scales had been banned, along with those ghastly shop-bought cake mixes, dahlin'!

We made party hats out of tissue paper, with glitter glued all over them (as well as all over the carpet!). By some interesting coincidence, we even found a 'Four' candle in a drawer, buried under a pile of decorations from previous years (oh Lord, I said, Four Candle, go on, say it, get it off your chest, you know you want to!)

The next decision was more controversial, but necessary to enhance the celebratory feel. Out of the three members of the Birthday Board, the youngest won and the other two had to stick Happy Birthday banners over paintings and doorframes. Yes, we're still talking about a blanket.

I checked that this was still normal behaviour with my WhatsApp group. The response from other parents was that it sounded pretty okay under circumstances, so I kept going, safe in that knowledge. Of course, I chose to ignore the winking / laughing emojis that accompanied their replies. Deep down, I knew they were all busy planning tea parties for comforters and choreographing Tik-Tok Teddy Bear dance-offs!

Now, back to the baking. Lockdown meant we'd just bought enough food to last for two weeks, which meant we had enough ingredients for shortbread biscuits and ricotta and chocolate chip cake.

I put flour, butter and sugar in a mixing bowl while music

played from my laptop, and proceeded to mix them by hand, quite possibly the best therapy against any lockdown blues. With the help of the aforementioned six-year-old, I worked the dough and gently shaped it into a ball, whilst singing to Crash Test Dummies followed by Ash and Radiohead.

'But mummaaaaayyyyyy … this music's boring.'

'I'm sorry poppet. There, let's stick on Paw Patrol on repeat,' I said whilst reaching for my earplugs. And the Amaretto.

As I turned around, I noticed my helper had deserted the kitchen, leaving a trail of flour and cocoa powder. I just hoped the trail didn't lead up the stairs.

Stairs clear.

Good.

Oh. Hang on, what were those handprints on the wall … and why did Thumbelina leave all those crumbs all over the bathroom sink?

Insert the abominable shrugging woman here.

Back to the kitchen, I shaped the dough into individual biscuits and arranged them in tidy rows on an oven tray. Hey ho, hey ho, it's off to the oven we go!

After a while the house smelled like a fun fair: sticky-sweet as candy floss and doughnuts, earthy as roasted peanuts, all in one.

For some time, the oven became a never-ending source of olfactory hallucinations; Alice in Wonderland meets Willy Wonka, possibly in Hansel and Gretel's witch's house.

I zoomed my mum and dad to show them the preparations. They asked me to call them again once the cake was ready so they could attend the party. I considered going viral with it, then decided to keep it in the family.

In the end, we immortalised the moment Blanket blew the candle. I would like to say no blankets were harmed in the process. Our Risk Assessment was watertight.

The picture showed Blanket with one of its corners propped up to look like its face, and another corner holding a plastic fork, with a plateful of cake and biscuits in the foreground. Unfortunately we didn't have time to buy presents, but Blanket didn't seem to mind. Which was gracious of it, taking into account we owed it five more birthday celebrations!

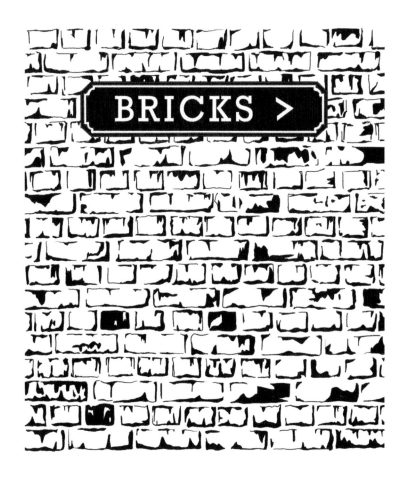

AULDBRICKAM

EILEEN DICKSON

In Reading Gaol by Reading town
There is a pit of shame.
And in it lies a wretched man
Eaten by teeth of flame

> — OSCAR WILDE, BALLAD OF READING
> GAOL, 1897

'MICHAEL, I can't believe that from a glorious choice of English towns you decided on Reading! All I can see is that it's an excellent station to get to other places from – we could be in Edinburgh in only eleven hours.'

'Helen, we've only just come from Edinburgh, and much as I know you hated leaving, the bank is actually in Reading where we live and I now earn our money.'

He looked carefully at her before pursuing the conversation. Her challenging tone seemed out of character with the calm, positive girl who'd thrived in foreign countries and uncertain absences.

'Darling, you knew the bank insists we move on after three years, and you've always adapted like a chameleon, but now we're grounded for a bit and you're feeling displaced. And cross.'

He was right as always. I knew I sounded contentious to my lovely husband who'd calmly put up with so much. We'd met at St Andrews and married shortly after he'd been gobbled up by bright graduate headhunters. Hong Kong, Toronto and Dubai followed, with me swimming happily in his slipstream. Not entirely happy: easing into high-rise glass buildings in cities where a medium 2.2 degree just about got me employment.

Travel and the stimulus of new people exhilarated me, but knew I should be doing more with my brain. Michael had immersed himself in his new job from which I'd sometimes felt excluded, but now it was up to me.

That Friday evening I'd made moussaka and garlic bread with a green salad. Red wine sat warming in its jug.

'Smells lovely Helen, are we expecting anyone?'

'Yes Michael, we're expecting the Return of your Wife, and about time, too; it's my challenge to explore Reading and what it's been known for, instead of sniping about it.'

'Well thank goodness for that. Now let's have supper, but I'll expect a Report.'

I enjoyed myself that week meeting people in the Museum and trawling through the Central Library for Reading's industries. The librarian told me that the town is known for its Four Bs: namely, Bulbs, Bricks, Beer and Biscuits. Scanning through Reading's history, I found it contained decades of enterprise, courage, resource and imagination.

I didn't include in my researches the famous Reading Abbey dissolved by Henry VIII in 1121; its lovingly restored ruins speak for themselves. Poor dead Henry I, the Abbey's founder, had been embalmed and sewn in a bull's hide for his return to the Abbey to be buried. His body waited out four stormy weeks in the channel from Normandy; there was scant respect for kings …

Huntley and Palmers – 1822 – Kings Road – Biscuits

Quaker Joseph Palmer started selling biscuits to stage-coaches travelling from London to Bath. Eventually they became the world's largest biscuit factory and supplied British armies and navies in both world wars. The best way to make these small 'hard as roof tiles' biscuits more edible was to crumble them to a paste and mix with hot stew or tea. A pater-nalistic company, they ran a sick fund but with strict rules. Fines were imposed and staff dismissed for misbehaviour. Guided by principles of honesty, self-discipline and hard work, whole families worked for them. Small boys were specially employed - not up chimneys, but lowered into 14-inch open-ings to pack biscuits into pretty tins for export. They ran their own volunteer Fire Brigade on loan to Reading Corporation if there was fire in town. Useful!

Simmonds Ltd – 1785 - Friar Street - Brewing

William Blackall Simmonds had fine ideas, commissioning his brewery from local architect Sir John Soane. He was malting his own beer in 1785. I warmed to this entrepreneur who waited until the licensing laws changed in 1830, allowing new public houses to sell ales. No surprise to find them supplying beer to the Royal Military Academy at Sandhurst. Nearby Aldershot was home to the British Army. Forging onwards Simmonds slaked thirsts in Malta, Gibraltar and India with lighter brews of India Pale Ales more suited to the climate. Soon the distinctive red hop leaf bottles were available on South East Trains. Sadly like the leaf, the company finally fell when they amalgamated with Courage and Barclay, and in 2007 the brewery moved further out of town.

By now, my attention span was waning; I'd been too engrossed in the other B's and still had bulbs and bricks to cover. Truthfully, I hoped there'd be less material than the others.

Suttons Seeds - 1777 – 1863 - Founded by John Sutton - relocated to Paignton

Their high-quality seeds and bulbs were sold to local large estates, and they were the first to supply seeds in foil packets. They earned a Royal Charter from Queen Victoria, who was generous with her patronage to several other companies.

This is excellent, I thought. I'll be onto Bricks in no time!

John Sutton in splendid black top hat and imposing whiskers. An idyllic print of a hay field with women in long skirts harvesting a hay crop from Suttons Grass Seeds. Sold as publicity posters, postcards and even jigsaws. The rural idyll was somewhat spoiled by a photograph labelled 'Traffic Chaos at Suttons roundabout.' Unnaturally quiet and not a top hat in sight.

My admiration for Reading's early entrepreneurs had

grown, but was it enough to sustain interest in The Report? I argued this wasn't to impress Michael but perhaps myself. Later, walking along the river path into town, sunlight played on a smooth wall by the Abbey ruins. Not just a wall, but the now immortalized Reading Prison. Biscuits, bulbs, beer and bricks may well be its heritage, but the Prison received Reading's most famous visitor.

Oscar Fingal O'Flahertie Wills Wilde

Oscar Wilde had taken over and absorbed everything else. However noteworthy Reading's past achievements, the Prisoner in Cell 33 was now my primary occupation.

Plundering information, I was transported to another time.

A time when from 1871, prisoners were kept in solitary confinement and allowed out only for chapel and exercise. During chapel they sat in special cubicles wearing a mask, giving no more than a view of bare feet. Forbidden to talk or communicate with anyone. Outside of solitary, a special cap with a thick veil was worn to prevent recognition. Many went mad.

When in 1891, William Watts stole cherries from a neighbour's tree and was sentenced to three days' imprisonment with hard labour. 10 years old.

When in 1892, Alfred Davis was sentenced to 21 days with hard labour and 12 strokes of the birch for stealing a rabbit. 11 years old.

The deprivation for Oscar Wilde was best expressed by his poetry:

I never saw a man who looked
With such a wistful eye
Upon that little tent of blue
Which prisoners call a sky

They were only allowed access to the Bible and Pilgrim's Progress, for those that could read.

It was impossible not to read further from what I now held in my own hands: Reading's rural past and prevailing judicial attitudes of the time.

<u>Executions at Reading since 1800</u>

29th March 1802 – Edward Painter – theft of two heifers

23rd March 1811 – Thomas Cox – bestiality

2nd August 1817 – James Castle – Sheep stealing

22nd March 1828 – Burnett, Field, White – shot game-keeper while poaching

11th January 1831 – William Winterbourne – robbery during Agricultural Riots

That span of thirty years should also include five murders, three forgeries and two burglaries.

Outside the sun shone through a clearing sky and I knew the Bricks had come to my rescue. In Jude the Obscure,

Thomas Hardy had christened Reading as 'Auldbrickham', the old brick town.

S&E Collier Ltd - Tilehurst

I seized the image gratefully. To medieval Tilehurst, the wooded hill where clay swung in buckets on aerial cables from clay pits. Walking through town, seen now with new eyes: elegant, blue grey tiles, pale golden and sand-faced, darker slate coloured, silver grey- facing bricks. Georgian and Victorian buildings of warm terracottas, so often taken for granted now revealed afresh and beautiful.

'Are you softening me up young lady? Michael asked after we'd enjoyed steak and salad that Friday evening. I poured us both a generous glass of Merlot. 'And now,' he said, 'the Report?'

I was reluctant. Nervous even. Found I was still absorbed in my research, unwilling to let it go. Now I wanted to share it with Michael, perhaps taking it further. 'Certainly not, but my original challenge was to explore Reading's history and discover what and who made it.'

'And have you succeeded, Helen?'

'Only partially: Biscuits have gone, Beer has gone, and Bulbs now growing in Devon. Brick makers also gone but their buildings remain when we remember to raise our eyes to look. And finally, Reading Prison - renowned for one man and his poem - is being sold.'

Seeing my animated face, Michael touched the papers in front of him. Refilling our glasses, he raised his own and said, 'But I have got my wife back.'

'Ah, better make the most of it darling, I'm going to be busy.'

LITTLE SISTER

STEVE PARTRIDGE

MY DAD SHOUTS up the stairs. 'Chrissie. What are you doing up there? Come down and watch Corrie with us.'

'I'll give it a miss tonight Dad.'

It's twenty-five past seven on a blazing July Friday evening in 1976, the hottest summer Europe has seen in living memory. I'm fourteen, and I'm laying as flat as I can on a pile of bed clothes squinting through my half open bedroom window. My window looks out towards a telephone box on the other side of a small green next to our council semi on the Oakridge Estate.

Mickey Gale and three of his mates are sat on the grass talking. Mickey is nearly seventeen and looks like Alvin Stardust. I like Mickey. He's got a lovely smile and he's always nice to me. There's a knock on my bedroom door. My Dad walks in. 'What are you looking at down there Chrissie?

He puts his hand on the window ledge, leans over me, and looks out of the window.

'Those boys are too old for you. And you need to stay away from that Mickey Gale. He's like his brother. Trouble'.

'He's always nice to me dad.'

'It's half time, the adverts are on, come and watch the second half of Corrie with us. It's just getting to the good bit.'

I look at my dad and screw my face up a bit. 'I like listening to the people in the telephone box. It's so hot they all leave the door open, and I can hear them talking. It's better than Corrie.'

'Don't let them see you. They won't like it if they think you're spying on them'. My dad goes to leave my room, turns, and gives me a look.

'What?'

'You know what. He's too old. And like I said, trouble'.

I screw up my face again and try to look my dad in the eye, but I can't. He leaves the room. I look back down towards the queue for the telephone box, Mickey Gale waves to me and smiles. I wave back.

Crazy Jane from number twenty-seven is shouting at her boyfriend down the phone. Pattie O'Brien is next in the queue. Pattie O'Brien is a thirty-something, a well-built white woman who looks like a rasta and talks with a Jamaican accent. She's wearing jeans, Doc Marten boots, has dirty blond dreadlocks and a ragged scar down her left cheek. She lives opposite our front door on the other side of the big green in Freemantle Close. She lives with three Rastas, two black and one white and her two mixed race daughters. The six of them live as a family.

Behind her is Schizo Di. Schizo Di's right hand is going up and down from her hip to her glasses every five seconds. Mum says it's a side effect from her drugs. My big sister Susan told me she had postnatal depression and smothered her baby. Sometimes she speaks posh. She lives with an older bloke.

Crazy Jane tells people it's her dad. Margaret's dad that is, not Crazy Jane's dad. Crazy Jane's dad is in gaol for armed robbery.

Pattie O'Brien looks at Mickey Gale and his mates sat on the grass. 'You got nothing better to do than sit about swilling beer?' As she says it Crazy Jane puts down the receiver and leaves the box. The phone rings almost immediately and Pattie O'Brien steps inside, picks up the receiver.

'Ello … Wot? Its Pattie … I'm not doing it for that. Seven fifty or nothing. Ok you do that. I'll wait five minutes, then I'm gone.' She bangs down the receiver.

Mickey Gale, my Mickey, is sitting on the grass with three of his mates drinking cans of lager and sharing joints. He looks at Pattie.

'You finished?'

'Get back to your beer, I'll tell you when I'm finished.'

'You're not speaking. The phone's down, I need to make a call.'

'Fuck off back to your can little man. This box smells of piss. Did you do that?'

'Fuck off rasta bitch.'

Pattie O'Brien steps out of the phone box and grabs Mickey Gale by his shirt collar and pulls him towards her. She twists his chin around with her left hand and makes him look at the side wall of our next door neighbour's house. The wall has a diagonal crack in the brickwork caused by the intensive summer heat running from the bottom left-hand corner to the top right-hand corner. Above the crack line to the left, painted in black is the legend 'SMASH THE NAT FRONT'. Five feet up the wall on the right-hand side of the crack sprayed in black paint on a red background is the legend 'NATIONAL FRONT RULES'. She points at it.

'Did you do that as well?'

'Wot if I did, bitch?

She pushes him away and at the same time kicks him in the groin. He falls to the ground groaning. I leap up and shout, 'Mickey!'

Pattie O'Brien looks up at me and glares. 'Draw the curtains, little sistren' The phone rings again. I duck down and listen.

'Pattie.' She listens for about thirty seconds. 'Six fifty or nothing, half first…call me Tuesday.' She slams the phone down and looks at Mickey laying on the grass holding his groin. 'You little shit.' She turns towards his three mates. 'Pick him up and fuck off. And don't be here Tuesday!'

She looks up but can't see me because I've drawn the curtains and I'm looking through the smallest gap from the left-hand side of the window.

Saturday evening. I'm standing outside of our front door listening to the music coming from the party at Pattie's house in Freemantle Close across the other side of the big green opposite our front door. Her small back garden is packed with people, drinking Red Stripe, smoking cannabis, eating jerk chicken, and dancing to reggae music. Bob Marley, Burning Spear and Peter Tosh are blasting out from two huge speakers made out of old wardrobes. The smell of ganja is all over the estate.

I hear my father shout to my big sister Susan. 'Find your little sister, bring her in and close the front door and the window. I'm not sitting here all night listening to the racket from that woman's house. When she's not selling dope, she's causing trouble. Social Services should take her kids and the police should lock her up and throw away the key.' Susan finds me on the edge of the green dancing on my own to the music and says dad wants me to come indoors.

On Tuesday morning I'm hanging out on the small green with Susan when a brick lorry arrives. The driver and his mate stack the bricks a few feet in front of our neighbour's wall. He tells us the council maintenance men will be coming next week to reinforce the footings beneath the wall and fix the crack with new bricks.

Susan tells me the word on the estate is that Mickey Gale's big brother Ronnie Gale is seriously pissed off with Pattie O'Brien for attacking his little brother and he will sort her for doing it. After my evening meal I leave Susan to watch Corrie with my parents and go up to my room at twenty-five-past-seven. As usual I fold my duvet in half longways and lay it under my open window. On top of the duvet, I put two pillows and my winter coat then I lay on top of the pile so I can both hear and see what is happening down by the telephone box. It's perfect; I can see outside without hardly revealing anything of myself.

Mickey Gale, my Mickey, and his mates are nowhere to be seen and there isn't the normal queue to use the phone. Right on seven thirty Pattie O'Brien walks across the grass towards the box. As she does, she glances up at my window. I duck down quickly so she won't see me. Then she opens the door of the phone box and steps back quickly as the stench of stale urine from inside of the box hits her in the face.

'Jeezuss!'

The phone rings. She lets it ring a couple of times then answers it.

'Pattie.' She listens for thirty seconds, then says, 'Ok six fifty. Three fifty up front. Sainsbury's café Basingstoke, ten thirty Saturday morning. In one of their bags. You be on time.'

She puts the receiver down and turns to leave the phone box. Standing in front of her are two six foot plus skinhead men in their twenties. They are wearing blue jeans, T-shirts, red braces, and bovver boots. The T- shirts have union jacks printed on them with 'N F' in the centre of the flag. The larger of the two is Mickey Gale's elder brother Ronnie Gale.

Ronnie Gale says, 'So rasta bitch, this what you do when you're not kicking the shit out of my little brother. Marrying illegals at six hundred and fifty quid a pop so they can screw Irish slags like you and live off the state.'

Pattie stares at him with her piercing blues eyes and says, 'Best you walk away now.'

Both of the men laugh loudly. 'And if we don't? What's going to happen exactly?'

Pattie looks to her right over the second man's shoulder. Walking out from behind the stack of bricks in front of our neighbour's wall are three men with dreadlocks and beards. Two are carrying knives, the third one who is wearing a black, red, yellow, and green hooped woollen hat has a meat cleaver in his right hand. The skinheads turn and look at the men walking towards them.

Ronnie Gale swivels quickly back towards Pattie, 'You slag,' and throws a punch at her. She pulls the door of the telephone box shut and he puts his right fist through one of the small glass windows. He tries to pull it out of the broken glass, but it sticks, and he can't release it. He shouts as it cuts into his hand and wrist. He pulls his fist back harder, shouts again, then jerks it out of the window. Blood is pouring from his wrist. He grabs his bloody wrist with his left hand and tries to staunch the flow of blood and at the same time looks to his right.

Standing three feet away from him is a short black man with dreadlocks and a kitchen knife in his hand. The black man eyeballs Ronnie Gale for a moment, then swipes him across the nose with the knife. There is a split second when nothing happens then his nose spurts blood. The black man is about to slash him again when Pattie shouts, 'Enough, leave him!' Pattie looks at the other skin head who has raised his hands in surrender to the third Rasta who is threatening to chop him with a meat cleaver. She points at Ronnie Gale. 'Help him.'

The second skinhead pulls a handkerchief from his pocket and presses it onto Ronnie Gale's bleeding nose. He pulls off his tee shirt, makes it into a tourniquet and ties it tightly around Ronnie's wrist. When the tourniquet is secure, he steps into the phone box and dials 999 for an ambulance.

Pattie looks at the three rastas, 'Come on. Out of here.' She takes the knife from the first rasta and points it at the skinhead in the telephone box. 'Ambulance! No Babylon! You hear me now! No Babylon!'

As she turns away, she looks up towards my window. 'Little Sister Chrissie, you up there? I know you are. You See Nothing! You Hear Nothing! You understand me now … I know you do, little sistren, I know you do!'

Ten minutes later I hear the siren when the ambulance arrives. Then I hear Dad running up the stairs. He knocks my door and bursts in at the same time.

'What's happening down there Chrissie?'

He leans across me and looks out of the window. Ronnie Gale is being helped into an ambulance by a medic. His skinhead mate who has blood all over his chest is stood back watching, shaking as he tries to light a cigarette.

'What happened, Chrissie?'

I look back at Dad, then I look over his right shoulder into the space left by the open door to my bedroom. I don't answer his question.

My father raises his voice. 'Chrissie, what happened?'

I stumble over my words. 'It was horrible Dad, horrible. Ronnie Gale tried to attack Pattie, cut his wrist on the telephone box door. Then he was slashed by another rasta, there were three of them, two with knives, one with a meat cleaver, hidden behind the bricks. Don't tell anybody what I've said, not mum, not Susan, not anybody. Pattie mustn't know I've told you.'

My dad looks at me. Hears the fear in my voice. Gives me a long look.

'Where are they now?'

'Ronnie was taken to hospital in the ambulance. Pattie and the rastas have gone.'

'And your friend Mickey? What about him?'

'Don't know, he wasn't there.'

My father gives me a look which says I don't believe you.

'He wasn't, Dad.'

'I want you stay away from him Chrissie. Don't talk to him. Any of them, they are all trouble. Promise me you'll do that.'

I look at my Dad, but I don't reply.

He shouts at me. 'Chrissie! Promise me!'

I say nothing and begin to cry.

THE BRICK FAÇADE

EMILY POWER

THERE's a handy opening question at funerals that never fails.

So, how did you know the deceased?

The questionee will open into a fumbled story that leads to more questions and before you know it there's a conversation in full swing. But other social events? Jesus.

I check my watch. 70 beats per minute, a bit high, and rising.

'So,' a short, well-kept man looks at me across the table of canapés. 'How did you get into bricks?'

My lucky stars, an opening line!

'Oh,' I swill my plastic champagne flute. 'You know; a childhood obsession with Lego.'

'Me too,' the man smiles, offering his hand. 'Mike Dormer. I'm only here for the spread.' He beams, taking another mini tart. These strained jokes flutter around the delegates at the National Brick Conference. Until two weeks ago, I couldn't have comprehended the existence of such a thing.

'Go to many of these, do you?'

Mike nods. 'Last one was cavity-wall insulation. There was a speaker who …'

I watch Mike's face intently, nodding along, with the occasional interjection to keep him talking while eavesdropping on the room.

'… And our shipment was delayed because of that …'

'… Please, Steve, the canapés are for everyone …'

There's another man standing lost, intermittently checking his phone, sipping the tiniest of sips with the most nervous of gulps. Interrupting Mike, I hold out my hand.

'Ryan Morgate,' I say. 'Director of Maplehurst Ltd.'

'James Walker,' the man says, 'Purbeck Ltd.'

'Tell me,' I say, trying out my line. 'How did you get into bricks?'

'Purbeck is *stone*,' James says, outraged. 'My uncle got me the job. He's the one who made me come here today.'

'Have you tried the salmon blinis?' Mike asks, and I leave the pair of them to it.

I prowl the room. It is a low-ceilinged conference hall at the University of Liverpool, with side rooms, normally for student seminars, where one-to-one meetings are being held. I skim the exhibitors' stands, trying to listen to the people around me while feigning interest in the leaflets, posters and brick samples.

'… Deborah from finance had never seen anything like it, I'm telling you …!'

'Care to join us?' Another man, this one white-haired and plump, enfolds me into a circle of men, and to my surprise, a single woman. They stand with wide grins and champagne glasses held with unease. 'I'm Geoff. What's your name and how did you get into bricks?'

'Ryan Morgate. I didn't plan to get into bricks …'

'Cory's the same, aren't you?' Geoff laughs. 'Just fell into it, or so he says.'

I've clearly walked into an in-joke because Cory bristles. 'I told you, I left school and it was just the first job I did.'

'Cory's never short for cash, are you Cory? We all think you're shipping more than bricks.'

'I'm not Gunnell,' Cory protests with disgust.

'Gunnell?' I ask innocently.

'Come on, Peter Gunnell, the guy who made a fortune importing bricks from Europe. He done the keynote.'

I shrug and smile. 'I wouldn't know, I just came for the spread.' They fall about themselves in forced delight. 'Which one's Gunnell?'

Geoff twists on the spot and points. 'Gent in the white suit. Classy as fuck, isn't he? Oops, shouldn't say that in front of the ladies.'

The one woman rolls her eyes. 'I don't give a shit, Geoff.'

I move on. I'm by Gunnell's side in a second; I can smell his hairspray. I turn to the nearest bystander.

'So,' the nearest bystander turns out to be a group of bystanders, all young and bemused by the situation they have fallen into. 'Ryan Morgate, Maplehurst Ltd. How did you all get into bricks?' They tentatively talk, thinking that I might be important, that I might somehow advance their careers. But I'm not even listening as I smile and laugh and say 'Oh, really?' and 'Wow, how fascinating!'

'… Can't this wait? We're at the Brick Conference, I've got to show my face …' Gunnell says.

'… We need to get going *now*, or we're done for …' It's a man's voice, and with a glance I see that he is wearing jeans and a jumper. At the National Brick Conference, no less!

To my horror, Gunnell is spooked by whatever's been said, and he moves twenty paces away. I usher my apologies to the young brick people and follow Gunnell, infiltrating myself into the next group.

My heart rate is 120 beats per minute.

'Hey! What a spread, eh? Ryan Morgate. How'd you all get into bricks?'

Gunnell snaps at his associate. 'Look, I'll make some calls, get the shipment diverted away from Mersey Dock.'

'We can't, that will look really bloody suspicious!'

'Better we look suspicious than get done, come on, let's make some calls.' And he's gone again.

'Sorry, lovely chat, got to run,' I say, disentangling myself from a discussion about the varying merits of English versus Flemish bonds, and I race after Gunnell, who bundles himself into the nearest meeting room.

I pause outside the door and employ my best loitering-without-looking-like-I'm-loitering tactic, which is to scroll mindlessly through my phone. I've twelve missed calls. I text my colleague: *Mersey.* And then I scroll, straining to hear. But it's no use. I can't hear a thing.

140 beats per minute.

I knock and enter immediately. 'Hi, are you Mike Dormer?' I say in my clearest, calmest voice. 'I've got a one-to-one meeting with you.'

Peter Gunnell has flames for eyes. 'There must be a double booking. We've got this room.'

'No, no,' I say. 'I've got an email confirmation. Just a second and I'll get it up,' and I return to my phone, with no plan but to stall, to stop Gunnell from making those calls. 'It was definitely here somewhere, oh wait, maybe it was my other email account.'

'Look, we'll just take another room, it's not a problem,' and Gunnell is off, his dressed-down associate tagging behind. They're out the door and heading across the conference hall towards the exit before I can think of another means of delay.

'Mr Gunnell!' I chase him. I follow him down corridors and through stairwells and out across the courtyard towards a bus stop where he has an Uber waiting. 'Mr Gunnell, there's no need to race off like that, I found the email and actually I was supposed to be in the room next door!' I come face to face with Gunnell and grin. 'You can have that room back.'

He is livid now, purple in the face, hopping from foot to foot. 'It doesn't matter, take the room, an emergency has come up.' He lunges into the cab. 'The docks, please.'

I'm only just quick enough to get into the front passenger seat. 'Oh, what a coincidence, I'm staying at the docks too! Let's split the bill.'

'Get out of the cab,' Gunnell seethes.

'Are you in one party?' The driver asks tentatively. 'Because if not you should probably get out.'

'Oh, yes we're together. We were just at the National Brick Conference, you must have heard of it, very big deal.' I say brightly, and the driver shrugs and sets off. I keep my eye on the road. 150 beats a minute. If Gunnell's got a weapon he's not drawn it. I can feel the back of my neck. There's not a peep out of Gunnell or his crony, just the faintest sound of frantic texting. I can only hope he's too late.

My watch buzzes and I look down. It's my colleague.

Got it. Hundreds of crates of hollow bricks, stuffed full.

I collapse against the headrest. 'Well, Mr Gunnell, the jig is up.'

'Driver, pull over.' Gunnell snarls, as we race along a major dual carriageway. 'I said pull over!'

The driver finds a bus stop. Gunnell and his man are gone before the wheels have stopped screeching.

I smile at the driver. 'They won't get far. Shall we carry on? I'm meeting some colleagues for a celebration.'

The driver is non-plussed and after a moment he tries an ice-breaker. 'So, how'd you get into bricks?'

'It's a new hobby, actually,' I say with a smile. 'Policing is my day job.'

I look down at my watch. My heart rate is dropping. 120, 110, 100.

Good job! It says. Bloody thing. It thinks I've done exercise. Still, it's more praise than I'll get from my superiors, so I take it.

KIDBRICKHOUSE

MEG WOODWARD

Window light, yellow on white
the quiet rings over crow squabbles
white, white, white
a makeup stain in the crease where she puts her head
to stop thinking.
Dust underfoot and thighs in the cold white draft
mint cold room, traffic breathes through thick glass
smashing her soul against duststacked jackets
the clock quarters three.

Feet together on the threshold and the door swings in
the carpet cream
and rotting
yellow damp underneath and the thin dark furniture
tangled bed
the shape of bodies in it
wallpaper peels brown as skin and the dust
is grey on the surfaces
light slides

between its curves.
Man-faced girl in the mirror trying to soften her own
    angles
built like a brick shithouse
she says of her.

Steps on the stairs – act natural
water falls behind the door and he breathes through it
bursting out
you alright dear?
White light on the marked toilet seat.
The floor is greengummed and the carpet's bones bite
when you step downward
to the sad horse one cornered
hanging on his rocked round feet
stitch tail on the wrong side of his anus.

Dark hall with the big brown door
big brown walls under greasy paint
shivered through shoulders
and the quartering clock
ticktock
her ghost could float on the sound of the clock and
the children playing outside.
Kid, brick shithouse they said of her
when she was young enough to disbelieve.

Dirty room
the deep carpet thick with dog
the collapsed dishcloth given up
spent

exhausted
and the hard cupboard full of compromises
tick tock pantry door squeaks
as she leans on it.
The clock counts down to three and
ends.

Kid in her brickhouse
old enough to bleed
but the smell of the house of her parents
is no stranger yet.
The garden looks soft from here but there is a sock
on the step
crumpled and dirty
left out for the rain
mud is trampled into the floor.

ACKNOWLEDGMENTS

Thanks to all the contributors who, as all writers should, put themselves and their finest work out there.

A huge thanks to Ilaria for our wonderful cover design, and Meg for pulling the whole thing together … and not forgetting Andy for keeping us all on track.

ALSO BY READING WRITERS

Voyages: A Reading Writers Anthology

Tales from our Town

See you for the next one!

Printed in Great Britain
by Amazon